"You're staying where I can keep an eye on you."

Maddox scooped her in his arms and deposited her in the middle of the mattress.

"Someone was prowling around outside the house. Care to enlighten me as to who it might be? No more lies. I want the truth."

She stared up at him, her eyes an icy blue, glistening with unshed tears. "I am telling you the truth. I do not know who is after me."

"You aren't telling me everything."

"I've told you what I can."

He turned away, afraid that if he continued to stare at her, he'd do something stupid—like take her in his arms and make love to her.

"I suspect you're a whole lot of trouble and we've only just scratched the surface." Tomorrow he had to convince her to trust him…if being next to her tonight didn't drive him crazy with need.

ELLE JAMES

HOSTAGE TO THUNDER HORSE

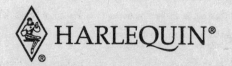

HARLEQUIN®

TORONTO • NEW YORK • LONDON
AMSTERDAM • PARIS • SYDNEY • HAMBURG
STOCKHOLM • ATHENS • TOKYO • MILAN • MADRID
PRAGUE • WARSAW • BUDAPEST • AUCKLAND

This book is dedicated to my new grandson,
whose arrival into this world was the best incentive
to get this book written. Happy Birthday, Cade!

Recycling programs
for this product may
not exist in your area.

ISBN-13: 978-0-373-69511-9

HOSTAGE TO THUNDER HORSE

www.eHarlequin.com

Printed in U.S.A.

ABOUT THE AUTHOR

Golden Heart winner for Best Paranormal Romance in 2004, Elle James started writing when her sister issued a Y2K challenge to write a romance novel. She managed a full-time job, raised three wonderful children and she and her husband even tried their hands at ranching exotic birds (ostriches, emus and rheas) in the Texas Hill Country. Ask her, and she'll tell you what it's like to go toe-to-toe with an angry 350-pound bird! After leaving her successful career in information technology management, Elle is now pursuing her writing full-time. She loves building exciting stories about heroes, heroines, romance and passion. Elle loves to hear from fans. You can contact her at ellejames@earthlink.net or visit her website at www.ellejames.com.

Books by Elle James

CAST OF CHARACTERS

Maddox Thunder Horse—Lakota Indian and North Dakota rancher, whose love of the wild horses of the Badlands leads to a winter rescue that turns into a long-term commitment to save a desperate woman.

Katya Ivanov—A princess framed for terrorism, on the run from law enforcement officials and a paid assassin.

Sheriff William Yost—The sheriff the Thunder Horse men despise for the slipshod investigation of their father's death.

Richard Fulton—A shadowy criminal who has eluded authorities for a long time.

Tuck Thunder Horse—Maddox's younger brother, the Federal Park Ranger in charge of protecting the North Dakota Badlands and its herds of wild horses.

Dante Thunder Horse—Maddox's brother, and helicopter pilot for the North Dakota branch of U.S. Customs and Border Protection.

Pierce Thunder Horse—Maddox's older brother, the one who left North Dakota to pursue a career in the FBI.

Dmitri Ivanov—Katya's brother, missing in Africa, next in line for the throne of Trejikistan.

Vladimir Ivanov—Katya's cousin, who covets the throne of Trejikistan and resents its move toward democracy.

Amelia Thunder Horse—Mother to the Thunder Horse men, who lost her husband to a freak riding accident.

Chapter One

He'd gained ground in the last hour, bearing down on her, the relentless adversary wearing at her reserves of energy. The cold seeped through her thick gloves and boots, down to her bones.

Alexi Katya Ivanov revved the snowmobile's engine, thankful that the stolen machine had a full tank of fuel. Regret burned a hole in her gut. Somehow she'd find the owners and repay them for the use of their snowmobile. She'd never in her life stolen anything. In this case, necessity had forced her hand. Steal or die.

She'd ditched her car several hours after crossing the border into North Dakota, and she was tired of wincing every time a law enforcement vehicle passed by. But she didn't know where to go. She'd only lived in Minneapolis since she'd been in the States. Instinct told her to get as far away from the scene of the crime as she could get.

Throughout the night, she'd pushed farther and faster, praying that she wouldn't be pulled over for speeding. Not until Fargo did she realize that the headlights following her hadn't wavered since she'd left Minneapolis. Butterflies wreaked havoc in her belly—whether they were paranoia or intuition, she didn't care. Her gut told her that whoever had framed her as a terrorist had also set a tracking device on the body of her car. How else had he found her and kept up with her through the maze of streets in the big cities?

She'd stopped once and taken precious time to search the exterior, but the snow-covered ground kept her from a thorough investigation of the undercarriage. Thus her need to ditch the car and find alternate means of transportation. Out in the middle of nowhere North Dakota, rental cars were scarce, if not impossible to find, not to mention they required a credit card to secure. She hadn't used a credit card since…Katya twisted the handle, gunning the engine. She refused to shed another tear. The bite of the icy wind was not nearly as painful as the ache in her heart. Her beloved father was dead. An accident, according to the news, but she'd gotten the truth from one of his trusted advisors back in Trejikistan. He'd been gunned down by an assassin while driving to their estate in the country.

Immediately after hearing the news of her father's death, Katya had been attacked in front of her apartment building. If not for the security guard she'd befriended, Katya would be dead. The same guard had hidden her from the attacker and let her know that the police had been to her apartment, claiming she'd been identified as a suspected terrorist. They'd found weapons and bomb-making materials there. Things that hadn't been there when she'd left to go to church earlier that day, hoping to find some solace over her father's death. The guard hadn't believed her capable of terrorism. Thank God.

On the run since then, she'd avoided crowded places, sure that someone would recognize her from the pictures plastered all over the local and statewide television.

She'd taken her car, switched the license plate with that of some unsuspecting person and driven out of Minneapolis as fast as she could.

Something slammed into the snowmobile, shaking her back into the present. A glance behind her confirmed her worst suspicions. The man following her had a gun aimed at her. For as far as the eye could see, there was nothing but gently rolling, wide-open terrain without trees, rocks or buildings to hide behind. The best she could hope for was to stay far enough ahead of the gunman to duck behind another hill. As her snowmobile topped a rise, another shot tore into the back of the vehicle.

Ducking low, she gunned the engine and flew over the top of the hill.

The ground fell away from beneath her, as the snowmobile plunged down a steep incline.

Katya held on, rocks and gravel yanking the skids back and forth during the descent into a rugged river-carved canyon. With each jarring bump, her teeth rattled in her head. Her hands cramped with the effort to steer the machine to the bottom. No snow graced the barren rocks, giving the snowmobile's skids little to grab onto. The rubber tracks flung gravel and rocks out behind her.

Katya couldn't worry about bullets from the man following her. It was all she could do to live through the ride.

With a bone-wrenching thump, Katya reached the riverbank. She couldn't believe she'd made it. She wanted nothing more than to throw herself on the ground and hug the earth.

Bullets pinged off the rocks beside her, forcing her

back into survival mode. She raced the snowmobile along the riverbank, aiming for the bluff that would block the bullets. The machine ran rough, the tracks slipping on the icy surface, getting less traction than needed.

With the shooter perched on the hillside, Katya was a prime target to be picked off. If only she could make it to the bend, her attacker would have to stop shooting long enough to follow.

Hunched low in her seat, she urged the hard-used machine across the snow and gravel. A hundred yards from the bend in the river and the reassuring solid rock of the canyon wall, it chugged to a halt.

Katya hit the start switch. Nothing happened. Bullets spit snow and gravel up around her. Katya flung herself from the seat to the rocky ground, crouching below the snowmobile. A bullet pierced the cushioned seat, blowing straight through and nicking the glove on her hand.

At the shooter's angle, the snowmobile didn't give Katya much protection. If she wanted to stay alive long enough to see another day, she'd have to make a dash for the canyon wall, where she hoped to find a place to hide among the boulders.

As if on cue, the snow thickened and the wind blasted it across the sky. She couldn't see the top of the canyon wall. And if she couldn't see all the way to the top, whoever was up there wouldn't be able to see her. Sucking in a deep breath, Katya took off, running upstream toward the bluffs.

The wind blew against her, making her progress slow, despite her all-out effort to reach cover. But once she was around the bend, the force of the wind slackened.

Katya hid among the rocks, bending double to catch her breath.

Her ride down the canyon wall had been nothing short of miraculous. Would the shooter make a similar attempt? Katya doubted anyone in his right mind would. Which meant he'd have to dismount and leave his machine at the top in order to come down and find her.

Without the snowmobile, she didn't know how she'd find her way back to civilization, but she could only solve one major problem at a time. Her temporary respite from being a target was only that. Temporary. In order to stay alive, she had to keep moving.

As she wove her way through the boulders and rocks, the wind picked up, the snow lashing against her cheeks, bitter cold penetrating the layers of GORE-TEX and thermal underwear beneath. Her feet grew numb and her hands stiff. At this rate, a bullet was the least of her worries.

The cold would kill her first.

MADDOX THUNDER HORSE topped the rise and stared down into Mustang Canyon to the narrow ribbon of icy-cold river running through the rugged terrain. He'd tracked Little Joe's band of mares to the valley below, worried about Sweet Jessie's newborn foal. Full-grown wild horses normally survived the harsh North Dakota winters without problems. But a newborn might not be so lucky. Temperatures had plunged fast, dropping from the low forties to the teens in the past three hours. With night creeping in and the snow piling up, Maddox couldn't look for much longer or he might be caught in the first blizzard of the season.

The handheld radio clipped just inside his jacket gave a static burst. "Maddox?"

Maddox fumbled to unzip the jacket just enough to grab the radio and press the talk button. "Whatcha got, Tuck?"

"I got nothing here in South Canyon. How about you?"

"Nothing."

"It's past time we headed back. The weatherman missed the mark on this one. *Wankatanka* grows angrier by the minute." Tuck attributed every change in weather to the Great Spirit.

The Bismarck weather report had called for snow flurries, not a full-blown blizzard. But Maddox had tasted the pending storm in the air. He understood this land and the weather like his ancestors, the equally rugged Lakota tribe who'd forged a life on the Plains long before the white man came. He'd felt the heaviness in the air, the weight of the clouds hanging over the canyons. Maddox knew if they were to find the horses, they'd have to hurry.

"See ya back at the ranch." Maddox clipped his radio to the inside of his jacket and zipped it back in place. Gathering his reins, he half turned his horse when movement near the river below caught his attention. With the snow falling steadily and the wind picking up, he had almost missed it. Maddox dug out his binoculars and pressed them against his eyes, focusing on the narrow valley below. Were Little Joe and his band of mares hunkering down in the canyon until the storm blew over?

Bear, the stallion he'd rescued five winters before, shifted beneath him from hoof to hoof, his nostrils flaring as if sensing the storm's building fury. Bear didn't like getting caught in snowstorms any more than Maddox did. The horse had almost frozen to death that winter Maddox and his fiancée, Susan, had been trapped in a raging blizzard. Bear had made it back alive. Susan hadn't.

Maddox peered through the blowing snowflakes to the bend in the river. His gaze followed the line of the waterway as it snaked through the canyon.

As a member of the Thunder Horse family, Maddox had grown up living, breathing and protecting the land he and his ancestors were privileged enough to own. Over six thousand acres of canyon and grassland comprised the Thunder Horse Ranch where the Thunder Horse brothers raised cattle, buffalo and horses. They farmed what little tillable soil there was to provide hay and feed for the animals through the six months of wicked North Dakota winter. For the most part, the rest of the land remained as it was when his people roamed as nomads, following the great buffalo herds.

Maddox loved the solitude and isolation of the Badlands. He'd only been away during his college days and a four-year tour of duty in the military. The entire time away from Thunder Horse Ranch he longed to be home again. The Plains called to him like a siren to a sailor, or more like a wolf to his own territory.

Now it would take an extreme change in circumstance to budge him from the place he loved, no matter what sad memories plagued him in the harsh landscape. Time healed wounds, but time never diminished his love for this land.

As his gaze skimmed the banks of the river, he passed over a flash of apple red. Orange-red and blood red he'd expect, like the colors of Painted Rock Canyon, but not bright, apple red. He eased the binoculars to the right, backing over the spot. Squinting through the lenses, he tried adjusting the view to zoom in. A white bump near the river's edge caught the blowing snow, creating a natural barrier quickly collecting more of the flakes. On the end of the drift, a red triangle stood out, but not for long. The snow thickened, dusting the red, burying it in a blanket of white.

Poised on the edge of a plateau, Maddox weighed his options. He hadn't found the mares and he still had an hour's ride back to the ranch house. If he dropped off the edge of the plateau to investigate the snowdrift and the red item buried in white powder beside it, he could add another hour to his journey home. In so doing, he risked getting stuck out in the weather and possibly freezing to death.

Instinct pulled at him, drawing him closer to the edge of the canyon, urging him to investigate. He rarely ignored his instinct, following his gut no matter how foolhardy it seemed. His army buddies called it uncanny, but it had saved his life on more than one occasion in Afghanistan.

No matter how cold and dangerous the weather got, if he didn't go down and investigate, curiosity and worry would eat away at him. He might not get the opportunity to return to investigate for days, maybe months, depending on the depth of the snow and how long the ground remained frozen.

With gloved fingers, Maddox tugged the zipper on his parka up higher, arranging the fur-lined collar around his face to block out the stinging snow now blowing in sideways.

He nudged Bear toward the edge of the plateau.

As they neared the dropoff, Bear danced backward, rearing and turning.

Maddox smoothed a hand along Bear's neck, speaking to him in a soothing tone, soft and steady over the roar of the prairie wind. "Easy, *Mato cikala*." Little Bear.

Bear reared up and whinnied, his frightened call whipped away in the increasing wind. Then he dropped to all four hooves and let Maddox guide him down the steep slope into the valley below. With the wind and snow limiting his vision, Maddox eased the horse past boulders and rocky outcroppings devoid of vegetation until the ground leveled out on the narrow valley floor. He urged the horse into a canter, eager to check out the mysterious red object and get the heck back to the ranch and the warm fire sure to be blazing in the stone fireplace.

His gaze fixed on the lump on the ground, Maddox pulled Bear to a halt and slipped out of the saddle. His boots landed a foot deep in fresh powder, stirring the white stuff up into the air to swirl around his eyes.

As he neared the snowdrift, the red object took shape. It was the corner of a scarf.

His heart skipped a couple beats and then slammed into action, pumping blood and adrenalin through his veins, warming his body like nothing else could.

He bent to brush away the snow from the lump on the ground, his fingers coming into contact with denim and a parka. His hands worked faster, a wash of unbidden panic threatening his ability to breathe. The more snow he brushed away, the more he realized that what had created the snowdrift was, in fact, a woman, wrapped in a fur-lined parka, denim jeans and snow boots. Her face, protected somewhat from the wind had a light dusting of snowflakes across deathly pale cheeks, sooty brows and lashes.

Maddox grabbed his glove between his teeth and pulled it off, digging beneath the parka's collar to find the woman's neck. He prayed to the Great Spirit for a pulse.

An image of Susan lying in his arms, hunkered beneath a flimsy tarp, while gale-force winds pounded the life out of the Badlands, flashed through his mind. This woman couldn't be dead. He wouldn't let her die. Not again. Not like Susan.

With wind lashing at his back and the snow growing so thick he could barely see, he didn't feel a pulse. He moved his fingers along her neck and bent his cheek to her nose. At last, a faint pulse brushed against his fingertips and a shallow breath warmed his cheek.

Relief overwhelmed him, bringing moisture to his stinging eyes. He blinked several times as he tightened the parka's hood around the woman's face and lifted her into his arms.

Too late to make it back to the ranch, he had to find a place to hole up until the storm passed. Being out in the open during a blizzard was a recipe for certain death. As he carried the woman toward his horse, he made a mental list of what he'd packed in his saddlebag.

This far into the winter season, he'd come prepared for the worst. Sleeping bag, tarp, two days of rations and a canteen. Trying to get the woman back to the ranch wasn't an option. Just getting out of the canyon would take well over an hour. Two people on one horse climbing the steep slopes was risky enough in clear weather. He couldn't expose the unconscious woman to the freezing wind. He had to get her warmed up soon or she'd die of exposure.

Maddox remembered playing along this riverbank one summer with his father and brothers. They swam in the icy water and explored the rock formations along the banks. If his memory served him well, there was a cave along the east bank in the river bend. He remembered because of the drawings of buffalo painted along the walls. He carried the woman along the river's edge, clucking his tongue for Bear to follow.

The stallion didn't look too pleased, tossing his head toward home as if to say he was ready to go back now.

The wind pushed Maddox from behind and for the most part he shielded the woman with his body. He crossed the river at a shallow spot, careful to step on the rocks and not into the frigid water. He couldn't get wet, couldn't afford to succumb to the cold.

The blizzard increased in intensity until he trudged through a foot and a half of snow in near-whiteout conditions. Maddox stuck close to the rocky bluffs rising upward to the east, afraid if he stepped too far from the painted cliffs, he'd lose his way. Bear occasionally nudged him from behind, reassuring him that the stallion was still there.

After several minutes stumbling around in the snow, Maddox thought he'd gone too far and might have missed the narrow slit in the wall of the bluff. A lull in the wind settled the snow around him, revealing a dark slash in the otherwise solid rock wall.

The entry gaped just wide enough for him to carry the woman through. Once the ceiling opened up and he could hear his breathing echo off the cavern walls, he inched forward into the darkness until he found the far wall. There he scuffed his boot across the floor to clear any rocks or debris before he laid her down in the cavern.

With little time to spare, he hurried back out into the storm to lead Bear out of the growing fury of the blizzard. As darkness surrounded them, Bear tugged against the reins, at first unwilling to enter the tight confines, his big body bumping against the crevice walls. When the cave opened up inside, the horse stopped struggling.

Running his hand along the horse's neck and saddle, Maddox focused his attention on survival—both his and the stranger's. If the woman had a chance of living, she had to be warmed up quickly. Although protected from the blizzard's fury, the cold would still kill them if he didn't do something fast. Once he came to the lump behind the saddle, he stripped off his gloves, blowing warm air onto his numb fingers.

Leaving the saddle on the horse for warmth, Maddox worked the leather straps holding the sleeping bag in place. Once free, he laid it at his feet on the cave floor. Next, he loosened the saddlebag straps and pulled it over the horse's back. Inside the left pouch, he kept a flashlight. His chilled fingers shook as he fumbled to switch it on.

Light filled the small cavern. The walls crowded in on him more so than he remembered from when he was a child. About half the size of the Medora amphitheater, the cave would serve its purpose—to shield them from the biting wind and bitter cold of the storm.

Without wood to build a roaring fire, they would have to rely on the sleeping bag and each other's body warmth—hers being questionable at the moment.

Maddox set the flashlight on a rock outcropping,

untied the strings around the sleeping bag and unzipped the zipper. He placed the open sleeping bag next to the woman. He had to get her out of the bulky winter clothing and boots and inside the sleeping bag.

Time wasn't on his side. He didn't know how long the woman had been unconscious or whether she had frostbite. Maddox stripped his coat off and the heavy sweatshirt beneath, wadding it up to form a pillow. Then he tugged his jeans off and the long underwear until he stood naked, regretting his lack of boxer shorts. The frigid air bit his skin, raising gooseflesh everywhere.

He went to work undressing the stranger, removing layer after layer. When he tugged off her jeans, she moaned.

That was a good sign. She wasn't completely comatose. Hope burned in his chest as he swiftly finished the job of undressing her down to her bra, panties and the pendant she wore around her throat. Nowhere in her pockets could he find any form of identification. He shoved all their clothing to the bottom of the bag, then laid the woman on the quilted flannel interior.

Tucked inside the sleeping bag, she didn't shake the way most cold people did. Her body had given up trying to keep her warm. The lethargy of sleep had numbed her mind to the acceptance of a peaceful death.

Maddox's body fought to live, his teeth chattering in the cool of the cave's interior. He refused to let the sleep of death claim her, as it had Susan.

Before he lost all his body warmth, he slid into the sleeping bag beside the woman and zipped the edges together. Although the bag was made for one large person, he was able to close both of them inside with a little room to spare. He wrapped his arms around her body, rubbing his hands up and down her cold arms and tucking her feet between his calves to warm them.

Cold. She was so cold.

Susan's face swam before him, her lips blue, her tawny blond hair buffeted by the wind, the only movement on her lifeless form. For a moment his world stood still as he stared down into the quiet countenance, the blank stare of his dead fiancée intruding into his thoughts.

But that was years ago. This woman wasn't Susan. For the first time since he'd found her, he studied the woman, blocking out the sad memories. In the shadowy glow of the flashlight, he leaned back enough to stare at the woman so near death he was afraid he might already be too late.

Dark hair, as black as his own, splayed across his gray sweatshirt pillow in large loose waves. Sooty, narrow brows winged outward in sharp contrast to her pale, almost translucent skin. Her hair dipped to a shallow peak at the center of her forehead and her lashes lay like fans across her cheeks. A pointed chin, perky nose and delicate ears completed her perfection.

As close as he was, Maddox caught a whiff of a subtle yet exotic perfume. His breath caught in his throat. This stranger didn't have Susan's girl-next-door fresh looks, yet her ethereal beauty was so profound it sucked the wind right out of his lungs, his groin tightening in automatic response to her skin against his. He hadn't been drawn to any woman since Susan's death. He hadn't let himself be, his burden of guilt weighing heavily.

The woman in the sleeping bag with him was a stranger. A beautiful, exotic stranger with skin the color of a porcelain doll and hair softer and silkier than anything he'd ever run his hands through.

He forced himself to focus on anything other than her physical attributes, shifting to all the unknowns, the mystery and reasons he shouldn't trust her. He didn't know her, she hadn't carried a driver's license or passport. He didn't know her background.

Who the hell was she? Would she live to tell him?

Chapter Two

Kat snuggled closer to the warmth in front of her, nestling her face into the hard, yet smooth surface. Her nose twitched and she slid her hand between her and the warmth-providing pillow, to brush her hair out of her face.

She couldn't move far with what felt like a tree branch draped across her back, holding her close and adding to the warmth. What was keeping her from moving? She opened her eyes to discover the source of her imprisonment.

Darkness so intense she couldn't see a scrap of light made her close her eyes and open them again. Was she dead? Panic shot through her like a lightning bolt. Had she gone blind? She shoved against the hard surface beneath her hands. The band around her waist shifted, tightening.

She pushed up on her hands, straining against the band. "Help." Her voice echoed as if in one of the large cathedrals of her homeland. "Where am I?" She fought to contain her terror. She had managed to stay alive based on sheer tenacity and by relying on her intelligence for the past two days. She couldn't give up now. But why was it so incredibly dark? Where was she?

"Shh." A deep baritone rumbled in the darkness, the surface beneath her hands vibrating. Then she was rolled to her side. She recognized the band around her middle now as an arm as thick as a small tree trunk.

Her heart slammed against her ribs. Had he caught up with her? Was she his prisoner? "Who are you? Where am I? Am I blind?" Her hip brushed against what could only be a man's… "Oh my god, you're not wearing any clothes!" She pounded against his chest, her feet banging against his shins.

"Slow down." The voice rumbled again, bouncing off the walls of the room they were in. "I'm not going to rape you, woman. Let me turn on the light."

With his one arm still holding her around her middle, he reached above his head. Cold air slipped across her skin, sending wave after wave of chills over Katya. She shook so hard her teeth rattled against each other.

Metal clinked against stone, then a click, and light bounced off what looked like rock walls.

Relief filled her as her eyes adjusted to the muted lighting. She wasn't blind. Light beamed across the room, dispelling the terrifying darkness. Then as quickly as the relief filled her it fled. She couldn't move, trapped against the man's chest and cocooned in a bag. Panic threatened to overwhelm her, but she fought it, taking deep, steadying breaths.

The man's other arm slipped back into the interior of the bag, pulling the gap closed, blocking the chilled air from leaking inside.

Despite her terror at being held captive, she didn't want to die of exposure. Until she learned more about the man she lay next to, she'd do well to appreciate the warmth and gather her strength if she had to fight for her life.

"How do you feel?" the man asked.

"Cold. Incredibly cold. And frankly, a little scared."

"You should be scared, but not of me. You almost died of exposure. You'll probably feel cold for a long time."

Her teeth chattered as she tried to form questions. "What happened? Why are we in this bag together?"

"I found you under a snowdrift by the river and brought you here to warm you. I only had one bag, so you had to share with me."

Her face burned. She stared around at the rock walls surrounding her. "Where are we?"

"In a cave."

"In what country?"

The man frowned. "The U.S., of course."

No *of course* about it. She'd been racing across the country for two days, never on a straight route, always varying her direction, hoping to shake the man following her. If the man currently holding her captive was one of the people after her, they could be practically anywhere. She took a deep breath before asking her next questions. "Who are *you?* Who do you work for?"

"Uh-uh." He shook his head. "You've been asking all the questions. It's my turn. Who are you?" His deep, resonant voice filled the inside of the cave with its ruggedness.

Katya hesitated. His avoidance of her question didn't set her mind at ease. She didn't know who she was dealing with and trusted no one with her identity. Especially after what had happened in Minneapolis. She'd been on the road ever since, until she'd been forced to ditch her car and steal a snowmobile. "Am I still in the Badlands?"

"Yes, ma'am. The Badlands of North Dakota, to be exact."

"My name is Kat," she said tentatively. At least she wasn't lying. Kat was only part of her name, but people she'd gone to school with in Minneapolis had used it as her nickname. "Kat Evans." Evans was an out-and-out lie. Hard lessons had taught her not to give out truth until she knew where she stood. Especially with the colossal accusation of terrorism hanging over her. Homeland Security, Customs and Border Protection, the FBI and every law enforcement agency would be on the lookout for her.

She squirmed against his body, extremely aware of her bare skin rubbing against his bare skin. He was completely naked and she was practically naked herself, except for her bra and panties. "Oh, my!" She tried to scoot away from him, hampered by the close confines of the bag they both occupied. A waft of icy air scraped across her body and she found herself pressing against his skin to re-create the warmth she'd felt a moment before.

"Sorry. You weren't awake for me to ask permission. In these temps, skin to skin is best to bring up body temperature the fastest. Yours was bordering on death."

After straining for a minute to keep from leaning into his chest, she gave up and let her cheek rest against the hard muscles of his smooth chest. "Well, then, I guess I should thank you for saving my life."

He chuckled. "Please, don't strain yourself with your gratitude."

With nowhere else to put her hands, she rested them against his chest, her fingers smoothing over the hard planes, liking his laughter and the contours of his muscles way too much. "Point made. I am grateful you did not leave me out there to die." She settled into the warmth of his arms, awkward about their nakedness, but too cold to climb out of the bag.

"You're welcome." He rested his chin on the top of her hair, a position both comforting and intimate. "Nothing like waking up in the dark with a stranger, huh?"

"Precisely."

"What were you doing out by the river on foot?"

She swallowed, hating that she had to lie to the man who'd saved her from freezing to death, but she had no other choice. "I was out snowmobiling and my snowmobile broke down."

The man stiffened. "What about the others in your party? Most tours stick together."

"I got separated. I drove around for a couple hours... trying to find them. That is when my machine quit on me." Her words came out in a rush as the lie grew bigger. What if he didn't believe her? What if he was the man who'd been after her and he was just fishing for more information? She couldn't let on that she was Katya Ivanov, just in case he really didn't know. Surely the entire United States had been alerted to a possible terrorist at large.

"I didn't see a snowmobile." His voice had hardened, as though he didn't really believe or trust her.

"I followed the river to see if I could find help. I suppose the snowmobile is a mile or so downstream from where you found me." She had hoped to hide it among the boulders, but had to abandon the heavy machine where it had come to a grinding and permanent halt, in order to save herself from a shooter's aim.

"The closest town to us is Medora and I don't recall anyone there offering snowmobile tours."

"It was a special tour out of…" she grasped for the name of a larger town in North Dakota. "Bismarck!" she said in a rush. How much bigger could the lie grow? And would she be able to remember all the details?

"Still, most tours wouldn't leave a rider behind."

"I am sure the weather cut them short on searching for me. I will bet they notified the authorities as soon as they got back. Assuming they did not get stranded too." Kat couldn't look into his eyes. Lying didn't come naturally to her, one reason she could never be a good politician. The question was: Did this man believe any of the lies she had just dished out?

"So really, who are you?" he asked, answering her question. "Kat Evans isn't right. You speak English too proper to have been born in America, and I detect an accent."

She stiffened against him. Like it or not, she couldn't tell him the truth. Not until she unraveled the mess her life had become. "I am from…Russia. And as long as we're stuck in this bag, can we leave it at Kat Evans?"

"Why? Are you wanted for murder or peddling drugs to children?"

"No. Nothing like that. I would just rather not talk about it."

"Running from an abusive husband? In which case, I'd offer a separate sleeping bag, but I don't have one."

"No. No husband." She stared across the cave's interior, wishing he would stop asking. "Is that a horse over there?"

"Consider him our chaperone. Bear is very good at keeping secrets. The stories he could tell, but won't, would shock you."

Katya laughed, although a little breathlessly. "I feel much safer, knowing he is here guarding my virtue." And he gave her a good diversion from the stranger's questions and naked body.

"Damn right." The man nodded toward Bear. "Don't tell her about the mare you stole from that stallion, boy. She wouldn't understand."

"I get it. You are trying to make me relax."

"You're brilliant as well as beautiful." His hand brushed against her hip. "Is it working?"

Katya's breath caught in her throat. The way his work-roughened fingers slid across her tender skin, aroused new sensations, making her body more alert, more sensitized to his nearness. "Somewhat," she lied, again. "I have never lain naked with a stranger before."

"That makes two of us. I usually get to know the women I sleep with *before* we climb into a sleeping bag together." His voice lost all hint of humor. "Short of freezing to death in a blizzard, we didn't have much choice."

A shiver wracked her body and she pressed closer to him, absorbing his warmth, her skin tingling everywhere it touched his. "Good choice." She inhaled the earthy scent of leather and male, noting the smoothness of his chest, not a hair on it. His nearness sparked a charge of electric current in her that made her want to explore more of his incredibly sexy body.

When was the last time she'd felt this drawn to a man? Never. The closest she had come was when she had been in lust with a politician's son back when she was nineteen. A time when all was right with her world and her country.

With her future a black hole of uncertainty and danger, how could she be this attracted to a stranger?

In the rock-solid confines of the cave, with the warm glow of a flashlight chasing away the severe darkness, Katya felt safe for the first time since she'd been on the run. Safe enough to think of something or someone other than simple survival.

With her body heating rapidly, Katya fought for something to break the tension and silence. "Is the weather still bad outside?"

"Listen…" He held his breath and cocked his head to one side. "*Wankatanka,* the Great Spirit, is angry."

Katya listened, concentrating on the silence. At first she heard nothing, then a thin, lonely wail whistled through the cavern, carried on a blast of frigid air that had found its way into their cocoon. Katya tugged at the edges of the bag, pulling it tighter around her shoulders, her face pressing close to the man's chest. "I suppose it's still bad out there." She snuggled closer, the lonely sound of the wind emphasizing the chill still present in her body. His warmth enveloped her and made her feel safe and nervous at the same time. "You still haven't told me your name."

"Maddox." His hand spread across her hip, his arm tightening, drawing her closer to his heat. "Maddox Thunder Horse. You're trespassing on the Thunder Horse Ranch."

"Maddox." She tipped her head up to stare into eyes as black as the cave when it had been the darkest. "Pleasure to meet you. Please accept my sincere apologies for the trespass." Her lips curled upward on the corners. "Thunder Horse is a different kind of last name."

"I'm a member of the Lakota Nation. My father's people were known for their strong horses."

"You are a Native American? Is the ranch on a reservation?"

"No, my father's father purchased the ranch from a retiring rancher fifty years ago. Since then, the Thunder Horses have added to the acreage."

As he spoke, his hand smoothed back and forth over her hip, climbing up to her waist and back to her hip, cupping her bottom.

The more he touched her, the hotter she got, her breath coming in short gasps as if she could not quite catch it. With nothing but her bra and panties between her and the large man holding her in his arms, all manner of wicked thoughts filled Katya's head. Her father would be appalled. "Do you have to do that?"

"What?"

"What you are doing with your hand?"

He jerked his hand away. "I was warming the cold skin. But if you're warm already, I can stop."

Immediately, Katya regretted saying anything. The heat his hand generated warmed her in many more ways than she could have imagined. "No, it felt nice. And I am very cold." And alone.

She could hear the echoes of her father preaching to her. Someone of her breeding should never find herself alone and naked with a man not her husband.

Sadness gripped her anew. The father who had driven her crazy with his archaic ideas of decorum could no longer dictate her life. Nor could he hold her in his arms and tell her everything would be all right. Boris Ivanov had been murdered two weeks ago, his limousine ambushed by a lone shooter taking him out in a single shot. The news reported his death as an automobile crash. Katya's inside sources told her otherwise.

A tear slid from the corner of her eye and dropped to the smooth skin of Maddox's chest.

He looked down at her, a frown drawing black brows together. His arm settled around her, his hand resting on her hip, his feet touching hers in the bottom of the bag. "What's wrong? Are you in any pain?"

He rubbed his foot along her calf, the warmth helping dispel the chill of her father's death. She shook her head. "No."

"I checked you over for frostbite. You looked okay a few hours ago."

She sniffed, disturbed in a very visceral, but not unpleasant way at the thought of Maddox inspecting her body while she lay semi-comatose. As his foot stroked her calf, she stilled her father's voice in her head, urging her to draw away. She liked the feel of his feet on her legs and especially his hand on her hip. A little too much for having just met the man. "I'm fine. Really."

"Then why the tears?"

"No reason." She sniffed again. "It's just..." sniff, "my father was mur—died." Katya sucked in a shaky breath and blew it out, attempting to pull away from the man's chest to keep from letting more tears drop onto his naked skin. Hadn't her father taught her better? Never let the public see you express untidy emotion. He had classified tears as unnecessarily messy. "I'm sorry. Ivan—" She bit down hard on her bottom lip and started again, struggling at lying to this man. "Evanses do not cry."

Maddox pulled her back in the crook of his arm. "I'm sorry about your father. I lost mine not too long ago."

Katya settled her cheek against his chest again and tilted her head up to study his face.

"I wish I could have said goodbye."

"Me, too."

High cheekbones, a rock-hard chin, dark skin and longish black hair gave away his heritage. The man could easily step into the past, hunting buffalo and living off the land. Again, his earthiness reassured her in the confines of the cave. He appeared to be in his element, completely capable of surviving in the harsh environment. Unlike her.

Having been raised surrounded by bodyguards, servants and political dignitaries, she had always relied on her social skills to survive. In the Badlands of North Dakota, social skills were less in demand and more of a hindrance. If she wanted to survive, she had better do as Maddox Thunder Horse said.

"How much longer do you think the storm will last?" she asked.

"Weather in the Badlands has a life of its own." He tucked the corners of the bag around them more securely. "Rest. At least, it'll pass time."

Although tired, Katya didn't feel even slightly sleepy. "I guess you are correct. Nothing else to do." Except feel his lovely body against hers. She never would have thought lying with a man could feel so good. With her nerves on edge, she could be awake for a very long time. Awake and aware.

He reached out of the bag toward the flashlight.

Her attention riveted on the light, Katya gulped. "What are you doing?"

"Conserving the batteries." He flipped the switch, plunging them into the inky blackness of complete and utter darkness. Katya's sense of sight consisted of the residual glow of the flashlight, fading as darkness settled around her.

Her body shook, her teeth chattering. Her fingers dug into his skin, the sensation of falling into an abyss making her hold on for dear life.

Maddox eased her fingernails out of his hide and laced his fingers with hers. "Don't tell me..." She could feel his head shaking back and forth over her head. "You're afraid of the dark."

"Sorry. It is a curse, something that has plagued me since I was very small."

"I can turn the light back on, but the batteries will eventually fade, and we might have trouble finding our way back out of the cave."

"Do not concern yourself about me. I will be fine." Trying to keep her teeth from chattering, Katya aimed for nonchalance, failing miserably.

Maddox's other arm tightened around her and he pulled her snugly against him. "Close your eyes and listen."

"What?"

"Just do as I say."

Katya squeezed her eyes shut, blocking out the cave's endless darkness. Now it was just her own darkness she had to overcome.

"Let me tell you a story my grandfather, James Thunder Horse, used to tell us as children." Maddox's voice hummed off the rocks, creating a warmth of spirit no heater or fire could generate. He spoke of a bear lost in the hills, trying to find his way home. Of a sly fox who led the bear farther away from home and a wise old wolf whose ferocity and courage helped the bear discover those virtues in himself. Ultimately, the bear found his way home, depending on the generosity of the wolf, and the assistance of the stars and the sun.

Katya's eyes remained closed throughout the story. Instead of relaxing, her body stiffened with increasing desire, each muscle and nerve intensely aware of Maddox, responding to the rhythm of his voice, the vibrations of his chest in a way she could not have imagined in the palace back home. "You have a gift." A gift possessed by no man she had ever met.

"It helps when you're lying naked with a stranger."

Katya could feel the strength in his body, the tautness of his muscles beneath her fingertips. She had never been this intimate with a man. Confined as they were in a cave, miles from everyone. Alone.

Even when she had explored sex with a classmate in the small school she had attended, she had not felt this close, as though their bodies melded into one.

Her hand slid across the hard planes of his chest, memorizing the texture and shape with her mind, imagining what it would feel like to love a man like this. To let him make love to her.

The heat in the sleeping bag intensified and her hand slipped lower. Would he be as hard all over? Her hand followed the ridges of his abdomen, sliding over the indentation of his belly button.

When her fingertips bumped into the steely velvet of his erection, a big hand caught her wrist, holding it in a vise grip.

"Don't start something you can't or won't finish," he said, his voice strained.

"I have never been with a man in a sleeping bag."

"Then maybe now's not the time to start."

"I must apologize. I cannot seem to help myself. You do something to me."

"You don't know me, and I don't know who you really are."

"What do you want to know? I am a woman. I am unmarried. I do not have any diseases and I am twenty-seven, old enough to make my own decisions." Perhaps she said the words to appease his conscience, but more likely the words came out to quiet her father's voice in her head. Either way, the words were for her more than him, and she recognized them for what they were. Permission to let go.

"Sex between a man and a woman takes two to decide."

He was right. Playing with Maddox Thunder Horse could be like playing with fire. But she wanted the heat he could provide, both outside and in.

Since her mother's death when she was only sixteen, she had been the perfect daughter to her father, playing hostess to foreign diplomats, always doing and saying the right things, never stepping outside the bounds of etiquette. "For once in my life I want to make a decision for myself. For me alone. Not for my father. Not for the people around me." She twisted her fingers around to lace them with his. "I know what I want." Then another thought sobered her. "Do you not find me attractive?"

He sucked in a breath and guided her hand to that part of him standing at stiff attention. "You tell me." His grip tightened on her. "If this is a tease, forget it."

Her hand closed around him. "I am stuck in a cave with a man I find very attractive and who obviously finds me not completely hideous. It is quite dark. We are cold and I am not teasing." She stroked her hand down his length, loving the contrast of velvet and steel. "Make love to me."

For a long moment Maddox hesitated. "This has to be wrong." His hand closed over hers, tightening her grip around him. Then he let go to slide upward to cup a full, rounded breast.

Katya's back arched, pressing her breast into his hand, hungry for his touch, for the feel of his lips against her skin.

Trailing his fingers over her breast to cup her chin, he drew her to him, bringing their lips within a hair's width of each other.

The warmth of his breath brushed across her lips and her mouth parted, a sharp draw of longing tugging at her core.

"I might regret this later, but for now…" His lips captured hers, grinding against her teeth, the force of his claim branding her with a desire so intense it stole her breath away. He moved against her, his sex rigid, pressing into her belly.

She shimmied out of her panties, while he unhooked the clasp on her bra. When she lay as naked as Maddox, Katya's legs fell open, letting him slide between her thighs. He eased her onto her back, settling down over her. Then he thrust into her long and hard, filling her, stretching her deliciously.

Their bodies melded into one, the heat they generated making their skin slick with sweat.

And she wanted more.

She raised her knees, her hands gripping his buttocks, driving him faster, harder, and deeper into her, until she lost all sense of time and place. They came together as two separate people, but now they were as one in body and spirit, riding a wave of sensation so intense Katya almost forgot how to breathe. As she plunged over the edge of reason, she let go of her worries, and clung to the present and his body.

Eventually, sleep claimed her, wrapping her in warmth and security. She was assured of her safety, if only as long as she remained in his arms.

Minutes, hours, days could have passed before she returned to earth, the floor hard against her back, an icy draft cooling her damp skin.

In a half-sleep state, she listened for sounds of the storm outside. Silence filled the dark interior. No wailing screamed in through the cave's rocky entrance.

With consciousness, reason and memories returned. A few hours ago she had woken up with a stranger, sharing his body's warmth, both of them practically naked.

Katya moved, her knee sliding down Maddox's leg, her bare thigh rubbing against his leg. She sucked in a gasp and her naked breasts pressed into his equally naked chest.

She had responsibilities. Her country needed her. Her people expected so much of her. And she'd just thrown it all to the wind to make love to a stranger.

What had she done? Would he understand when she had to leave? For leave she must, just as soon as she could contact her government for help. Katya chewed on her lip, her brow furrowing. Having ditched her car, and lost her identification and credit cards back on the snowmobile somewhere along the river, getting help would definitely be a challenge.

Chapter Three

Maddox lay beside the woman, guilt gnawing at him. He'd made love to a stranger not quite two years since the death of his fiancée. Susan, who'd grown up in the Badlands, who knew the dangers of living on the prairie, who loved the land and wild horses as much as he did. His perfect match in every way. And in every way so different from the woman lying in his arms.

Susan's sun-kissed tawny hair reminded him of wheat and late-summer prairie grasses, wispy and straight, always blowing in the wind. Her eyes as gray as a storm-filled sky. Her long, lanky body strong and adept at riding the range alongside him.

Kat was nothing like Susan. Her hair lay in a mass of long, loose, black curls, emphasizing her pale skin and eyes as light as his were dark. Her diminutive body, though small, had curves that fit perfectly in his palm, a fact that brought on yet more twinges of guilt. How could he compare them? Susan had been his life, his soul mate, the woman he'd planned to spend the rest of his life with. Only her life had ended and he'd resigned himself to continuing on alone.

Yet this dark-haired beauty, with hands so soft they couldn't have worked a hard day's labor her entire life, lay naked against him. The smell of her skin, the softness of her body, still made him hard as a rock.

Maddox stiffened, his hands dropping to his sides, his fingers burning as though on fire from touching her. He jerked the sleeping bag's zipper down, a frigid blast of arctic air biting at his naked flesh. He reached for the flashlight and switched it on.

Kat blinked, her eyes widening as the cool air hit her skin and pebbled the tips of her breasts. "What's the matter?"

"Nothing." Before he changed his mind and claimed her, Maddox climbed out of the bag, reaching back inside for his clothing lodged at the bottom.

In the freezing interior of the cave, he dressed quickly, fully aware of Kat's gaze watching him, and thankful for the effect of the frigid temps on his libido.

Kat pulled the bag up to her nose, her dark eyes rounded, each breath a puff of steam. "Did I do something to make you mad?" She laughed. "I apologize. I have never been this forward with a man. I'm not usually left alone with one long enough." Her eyes widened and she clamped her lips shut.

Maddox slipped into his insulated trousers, buttoning the fly. "Dress inside the bag. We leave as soon as it's daylight."

"Leave?" She shrank deeper into the bag, a tremor shaking her cocoon.

"Yes, leave." Her big eyes reminded him of a scared colt, and he almost softened. Instead, he turned on his heels and edged through the crevice out into the bitter-cold wind.

The sun hovered below the horizon, giving the landscape a steely, washed-out, gray-blue glow. Clouds clogged the sky in a blanket of charcoal-smeared waves of dirty white, churned by the ever-present wind.

Maddox braced himself before leaving the relative shelter of the tumbled boulders to stare up the hillside at the icy terrain. They'd have to climb the rugged sides of the canyon wall to reach the plateau. From there it was an hour's trek on horseback to the ranch house.

As bitter cold and windy as it was, he preferred to get back to the ranch rather than spending another night in the sleeping bag with Kat Evans—or whoever she really was. The sooner he got back, the sooner he could relinquish his responsibility for the woman.

Maddox unclipped the radio from his jacket and flipped the On switch. "Tuck, you out there?" As he waited for any response, he knew he'd get none. The handheld radios had a short range. More than likely, Tuck had made it back to the ranch and was wondering what had happened to Maddox. He hoped they hadn't sent out a search party. With the skies as heavy as they were, they could be in for another onslaught of the white stuff.

Maddox closed his eyes and drew in a deep breath, the frigid air stinging his lungs. He could taste the coming snow, feel it in his blood, chilling him to the bone. It would arrive soon. Too soon for comfort.

Something touched his arm, jerking him out of his trance and back to the canyon floor. He spun, braced for attack.

Kat stood with her arms crossed, the red scarf wrapped around her nose and mouth and her jacket hood pulled up over her hair. Buried in all those layers, her pale face peeked around the edges of clothing, her eyes as wide as icy-blue saucers. "I am r-ready," she said, her voice muffled by the wool scarf.

"Then we leave." He reentered the cave, making quick work of rolling up the sleeping bag. Flashlight in hand, he led the stallion through the entrance and out into the windy gray of predawn.

Kat waited at the cave entrance, stamping her boots in the snow, rubbing her hands along her arms, her gaze darting from side to side as if she feared venturing out for more reasons than the cold wind. "Are you sure we shouldn't stay here?"

One look at Kat and the memories of the night before hit Maddox like a sucker punch to the groin. "We move." He didn't ask permission or warn her. With little effort, he grabbed her around the waist and swung her up into the saddle.

Kat squealed and held on to the saddle horn as Bear reared and danced to the side.

She sat the horse well, despite his nervous dance, as though she'd ridden before. A woman with soft hands who could ride.

Maddox tucked that little bit of insight away in the back of his mind. He'd get to the bottom of Kat Evans when they were safe from the weather. With gentle hands, he pulled on the reins, running gloved fingers over the horse's nose, speaking to him in Lakota, calming him.

Then he set out at a quick pace, leading the horse along the base of the bluffs, searching for a suitable path to climb out of the canyon.

"Aren't you going to ride with me?" Kat called out, hunkered down as low as she could get in the saddle to escape the full force of the driving wind. Her voice barely carried over the roar of wind bouncing off stony cliffs.

"Not until we're out of the canyon." Finally, a break in the sheer rock wall revealed a narrow path zigzagging up the side of the canyon, probably left by elk or big horn sheep. Maddox climbed the hill, the horse close behind him. Kat clung to the saddle horn as they rose from the riverbed up the treacherous trail.

Several times Maddox's boots slipped on loose rocks, sending a tumble of gravel and stones toward the horse. Bear sidestepped and almost lost his footing. Kat's hand flailed out for balance, her face even more pale and pinched than when they'd started up the incline.

Maddox found that the less he looked at her, the better he felt. Only when he had to did he turn to make sure that she hadn't lost her grip and fallen from the horse.

Kat's fingers and cheekbones burned with the cold. Not long after they left the cave, she started shivering and could not seem to stop. She could not afford to waste all her energy, not when she had to use all her strength just to hang on.

She cast a look over her shoulder to the canyon floor, wondering where the man who had been following her had gone. Had he headed back when the storm struck? Or had he holed up as she had? In which case, he would be out looking for her again.

A shiver shook her so hard her teeth rattled. If not for Maddox, she would have died out there, saving the man following her the trouble of killing her.

Where would that leave her country? Without a ruler, without anyone to lead them into democracy, her people would fall back into chaos and warlords would take over. She needed to find out who was behind her father's death. No matter what the news reports said, that car crash had begun with a bullet. A deliberate attack by a skilled assassin.

Whoever was after her did not plan on holding her hand and escorting her back to her country. He had taken several shots at her before she had lost him. Skimming through streams and across barren rocks had taken their toll on her snowmobile, but had bought her much-needed time to escape in an otherwise snow-covered landscape.

She had taken a huge risk crossing Minnesota and North Dakota in a car. The open farm fields and grasslands left little cover and concealment. But she kept moving just to escape the law and the predator tailing her. Only he had been persistent and tracked her every move. She was tired of running, tired of always looking over her shoulder, completely cut off from everyone who could possibly help.

As they climbed higher, the terrain became increasingly more treacherous and their footing more precarious. The more Kat looked back at the canyon floor, the dizzier she got. The canyon wall inclined at more than a forty-five-degree angle, the path they followed less than six inches wide in most places. How she longed to be on foot, rather than perched high on a horse's back, even that much farther from the ground.

Nausea fought with vertigo, making her head spin. Kat squeezed her eyes shut and clung to the saddle horn. Because the stirrups were so long, her feet did not quite reach the footrests, giving her no way to balance her weight on the big animal. With her hands quickly freezing and the possibility of a frightening fall making her hold tighter, she thought the ride to the canyon's rim would never end.

With one mighty lunge, the horse nearly unseated her, clearing the edge of the canyon and arriving on the plateau above.

Kat opened her eyes, the wind whipping her scarf across her face. For as far as she could see, semi-barren rolling hills stretched before her.

Behind her, the canyon cut a long, jagged swath out of the prairie walls blown free of snow, glowing a ruddy red in the increasing light from the muted sun. Every breath of the wickedly cold air stung her lungs and bored through her thick clothing. Chills shuddered across her body and she huddled lower in the saddle, praying for the journey to end, preferably in a hot tub. She groaned. How she would love to sink neck deep into a warm bath and stay there until her skin shriveled.

All the while she had been perched atop the giant stallion, Maddox had been climbing the hill. He had to be tired by now. Was he as cold as she was? Did he wish to be done with this trek—and her?

Several hundred feet from the rim of the canyon, Maddox stopped to catch his breath and speak to the horse in a language Katya did not understand. She assumed he spoke the language of the Lakota Nation.

In the light, she could finally see him. Dark skin, black eyes and straight, thick black hair falling to his shoulders. He tugged his fur-lined parka up around his face and turned to face her.

With the ease of one born to ride, he placed one foot into the stirrup and swung up onto the horse's back, landing behind the saddle.

His arm wrapped around her waist and he lifted her,

easing himself into the seat beneath her, settling her onto his thighs.

Immediately she could feel his warmth through her clothing. Just blocking the wind on one side made a difference. She sank back against him, glad for his presence and the balance he provided on the moving beast.

He did not say anything and with the wind so strong it could steal her breath away, Kat did not speak either.

For several miles, they rode in silence, curled into each other.

The gentle rocking motion of the horse, plus the constant cold, lulled Kat into a dull, half-sleep state. Snow turned to sleet, the tiny hard pellets slung sideways by the approaching storm.

"Don't go to sleep, Kat Evans," a voice said over the roar of the wind.

"Why?" she leaned against him, her eyelids dropping over snow-stung eyes. "I am exceedingly tired."

"If you fall asleep, who will I talk to?"

She snorted softly. "You were not talking." She turned her face into his jacket. "I am so cold."

"We'll be there in less than half an hour."

"I need to sleep."

"Talk to me, Kat," he said, his chest rumbling against her back.

"About what?" she muttered, her eyes closed. She had to keep her secrets, but she didn't have to stay awake, did she?

"How did you get into the canyon? We're miles from the closest highway or public lands."

In her sleepy haze she could not think straight. How much could she reveal? Did she care? She gave a half-hearted attempt at laughter and opted for mostly truth. "I did not see the canyon. I drove my snowmobile over the edge. It did not stop until it reached the bottom beside the riverbed."

Funny how leaning against Maddox, with the soft swaying of the horse beneath her, lulled her into thinking the horrible tumble down the bluff was nothing but a bad dream. Except for a few bruises, she had survived, only to fall victim to the extreme cold and mind-numbing lethargy.

Other than her hands and feet, she was fairly warm in Maddox's capable arms. They did not build men this rugged where she was from. Her brows furrowed. Or she had never met any men who had been built this sturdy. Her father had kept her surrounded by bodyguards and state officials everywhere she went in Trejikistan.

Maddox shifted her weight, pulling her closer against him. "Why were you snowmobiling out this far? Why not closer to Bismarck?"

"Cars cannot follow." She yawned and settled back against him, her eyelids closing for the final count. "Unfortunately other snowmobiles can."

"Isn't that the idea with a snowmobile tour?" Maddox's words were carried away on the wind as Katya slipped into a numbing sleep.

Maddox stopped the horse periodically to tuck Katya's hands into his jacket and adjust her position to keep her from getting too cold in any one place. As he rode Bear through the storm, he went over Kat's words again and again. They didn't make any sense. Had she been out on a snowmobile tour and gotten lost? And what did she mean that cars couldn't follow but snowmobiles could? Had she been running away from something? Was someone following her?

Maddox vowed to get to the bottom of it all when they finally made it back to the ranch. The one-hour ride from the canyon rim stretched into two as the storm settled in around them.

Sleet turned to snow, blowing in sideways, making it difficult for him to see more than two feet ahead of them. At one point, he took shelter in a ravine, the wind and sleet too harsh to be out on the open plains.

Too cold to remain exposed much longer, he ventured out again, hoping Bear knew the way. Maddox couldn't make out any landmarks and the storm only grew worse, nearing blizzard conditions.

Maddox hoped the horse's sense of direction led them back to the safety of the barn and ranch house and not farther away.

When he'd just about given up hope of getting there, the ranch house materialized through the whiteout conditions.

A dog barked, and a light blinked on next to the front door.

Through the driving snow, his brother and a ranch hand raced out into the blizzard toward the horse and the two people sagging in the saddle.

"Take the woman." Maddox handed Katya down into waiting arms. He didn't like others carrying her away, but the cold had taken more out of him than he originally thought.

He nudged the horse toward the barn. When they reached the barn door, he slipped from the saddle, his legs buckling. If not for the horse standing beside him, Maddox would have gone down in the snow.

Three Thunder Horse ranch hands emerged from the barn. One took the horse's reins and the other two rushed to grab Maddox's arms, draping them over their shoulders. His horse taken care of, Maddox let the men walk him up to the house. Once inside, he settled in a chair near the hearth where a fire blazed with enough warmth to thaw even the coldest parts of his body.

His mother, Amelia Thunder Horse, crouched on the floor in front of him and tugged his boots off his feet and the socks with it. "Thank the Lord you made it back. We were so worried. Who is the woman you brought with you? Where did you find her?"

Too tired to answer her, Maddox stood. "I'll answer all your questions later. Where is she?"

"In the guest bedroom."

Maddox stumbled down the hallway, shedding his jacket. When he reached the guestroom, Mrs. Janek, the housekeeper had just finished tucking Kat into the bed, the blankets drawn up to her chin. The older woman clucked her tongue. "She's out. I hope she'll be all right. Do you want me to call the doctor?"

"No, I'll see to her." Maddox stood next to the bed, staring down at the woman who'd called herself Kat. In his gut, he knew she hadn't told him the entire truth. Despite that, he couldn't help the overwhelming need to protect her that came over him.

Tired beyond endurance, he pulled the covers aside and lay in the bed beside her, gathering her into his arms as he'd done in the cave.

"Maddox?" His mother hovered in the door of the guestroom. "Is she okay?" She twisted her fingers together, her brows dipped in a worried frown. "Are you okay?

His eyelids weighed so heavily, he closed them. "I don't know, Mother. Somehow, I don't think I'll ever be okay."

Chapter Four

Lights glittered in the myriad chandeliers hanging from the vast ceiling. Too bright, all merging and blending together as she spun around the room, dancing from partner to partner. In a deep red ball gown, her hair piled high on her head and the world at her feet, Katya smiled, laughed and drank champagne from crystal goblets.

At one point her father danced her around the room. She was a little girl all over again, smiling up at him, proud of the man who ruled Trejikistan and made her feel loved and protected. So relieved to see him healthy and happy, she leaned against him and hugged him tight. "They told me you were dead."

He just laughed and spun her into the arms of her brother, Dmitri, so tall and handsome, his wavy black hair so much like her own. His hands held her, gently guiding her through the steps of the intricate traditional dance of her ancestors. Hands of a doctor, a man meant to do good for the people, with a heart so big he could love every child in their country.

Katya smiled and laughed at him. "Where have you been, Dmitri? We have all been so worried."

Before he could answer, the music ended. Dmitri

tweaked her nose, just as he had since she'd been a small child, and disappeared into the crowd.

Standing alone in the crowd of guests, Katya looked around for her father and brother, suddenly sad, lonely and afraid. The orchestra played a waltz, the music so beautiful it melted Katya's fears and sadness away. As she glanced around the ballroom, the sea of blurred faces parted and one man stood at the center. Unlike the other guests, this man didn't wear a tuxedo or the uniform of a military man. He wore buckskins and moccasins, his long black hair hanging down around his shoulders, a wild gleam in his brown-black eyes.

As if drawn to him by a magical thread, Katya floated across the room toward him, the other guests fading away in a haze of gray. She could see his face so clearly, every line, angle and shadow etched in her memory. When the tall, swarthy Lakota native took her in his arms, he moved with the grace of a lion. At ease in his traditional dress, he waltzed her around the room, ignoring the whispers and comments made by statesmen and their wives, oblivious to the pomp and circumstance strictly adhered to in formal settings.

For once, Katya did not care that she might not fit in, that the man she danced with would draw censure from the exalted guests. Princes, princesses and leaders of foreign countries did not matter to her as long as she remained in the Lakota native's arms. The world didn't exist, except for the two of them.

As the music faded to a halt, the world crowded in. Her father gripped her arm and pulled her away from the Lakota.

"No!" she cried out. "I want to stay with him."

But her father's grip tightened and he led her out

of the palace and into a waiting limousine where her brother sat, shaking his head.

"No! Let me stay. I want to dance," Katya called out.

The limousine sped into the darkness, the lights from the palace fading with each passing mile. Katya looked back, her tears blurring her vision.

When she slumped into her seat beside her father and brother, she could not stop sobbing. "Why?"

Suddenly, the vehicle lurched, rammed by another car speeding along the highway. The limousine spun around and around, the motion flinging Katya around the inside. Out of control, it pitched over the edge of the road and tumbled into a ditch.

The door nearest her flew open and Katya fell into the ditch, facedown, her beautiful gown ruined in the mud.

She lay for a moment, wondering if she had died. But the sticks poking into her hands and face made her open her eyes and look around.

The limousine lay on its side, riddled with bullet holes.

"No!"

MADDOX HAD AWAKENED WHEN Kat first kicked out in her sleep. He stared down at the woman who'd managed to end up in his arms yet again.

Her brows dipped together and a tear slipped down her cheek, even as she slept.

What was he doing? What happened to the plan of dumping her on someone else as soon as they reached the ranch house? She wasn't his problem and he didn't want to be responsible for her.

Deep in a terrible nightmare, she cried out.

And despite his determination not to care, his heart went out to her. She must have gone through a lot, getting lost from her tour and falling into a canyon—not that he completely believed that story. If he hadn't come along when he had…it didn't bear thinking about. He couldn't erase the image of her lying in the snow, her face so pale. He could forgive her lies, but he couldn't forgive himself if she'd died. "Kat, wake up."

"Dmitri, don't go!" she mumbled. "I need you."

His chest tightening, Maddox shook the woman. "Wake up." Who was Dmitri? Kat had told him that she was single. He didn't make love to married women. Or even those promised to another man. Too much about Kat Evans remained a mystery, and Maddox didn't like it when he couldn't get to the bottom of things. An unexpected surge of anger powered through him. "Kat!"

Her eyelids fluttered, then opened. "What? Who?" Her gaze shifted around the room and returned to his. "We are not in the cave." She closed her eyes again and leaned her face against his chest.

A knock on the door drew his attention away from the black-haired beauty lying so naturally in the crook of his arm.

Maddox's mother pushed open the door, balancing a tray in her arms. Amelia Thunder Horse smiled. "You two missed dinner, so I brought it to you. And we have company."

Maddox frowned. "In this weather?"

His mother's smile widened. "You've been asleep for several hours." She set the tray on a table and scooted it close to the bed. "It stopped snowing, and the wind is dying down." Amelia planted fists on her hips and stared directly at Maddox and Kat. "Are you two going to sleep the rest of the night away, or are you going to eat some of this food I slaved over?"

Kat sat up, her eyes wide, her face flushing a rosy red. "I beg your pardon." She slipped out of the bed and stood in the rumpled shirt and jeans she'd arrived at the house in. "Is there someplace I could wash up?" She shoved her mass of black hair away from her face. "I must be a fright."

"Of course." She led Kat to the bathroom. "In here. I'll bring a change of clothes in a minute."

Maddox's stomach rumbled as he sat on the edge of the bed and reached for a fork, painfully aware that he'd gone an entire day without eating. "Who's the company?"

His mother picked up Maddox's discarded shirt, refusing to meet his gaze. "Sheriff Yost."

Without taking the bite of food, Maddox slammed his fork down on the tray, rattling the plates and glasses. "What the hell's he doing here?"

Amelia Thunder Horse shrugged. "Checking on us after last night's storm."

"And is he checking on every other rancher in the county as well?"

"I didn't ask him." She faced Maddox. "He'd like to talk to you and your visitor."

Maddox's eyes narrowed. "What does he know?"

She shook her head. "No more than any of us."

"How does he know she's even here?"

"Tuck mentioned it. The sheriff probably just wants to notify her family that she's all right."

Kat stepped through the door of the bathroom, her

fingers attempting to comb her hair into place. "Whose family?"

"Yours, dear." Amelia smiled and crossed the room. "I'll get a brush and those clothes I promised. You have a lovely accent."

"Mother—" Maddox stood, intending to tell his mother just what he thought of Sheriff Yost, but she cut him off with a stern look.

"Maddox Thunder Horse, you'll speak with the sheriff and you'll be nice." She shot a wry smile at Kat and left the room.

Kat stared across at Maddox, her eyes wide, worried. "I don't have a family for him to notify."

"So you say."

"You don't believe me," she said, her words flat. "Are you going to turn me over to the sheriff?"

"Have you committed a crime?"

"Well…" Her frown deepened.

"Why do I have a feeling that this situation is going to get even more complicated?"

"Because it will." She gave him a weak smile. "I do not have any of my documents on me. I am a foreign national, and I lost my visa and all my identification papers back on the snowmobile in the canyon."

"Convenient."

"I have copies stored in a safe place, if I can just get to them."

"Or you could contact your embassy and have them forward them to you."

She nodded, not really answering or committing to his suggestion. What was it she held back? What was she not telling him?

"Look, whatever trouble you're in, you might as well tell me now. I don't like being blindsided."

"You would not understand," she said, her back stiffening. "You might as well turn me over to the sheriff now. I'll go quietly." She faced off with him, daring him to do just what she suggested.

For a moment, he considered it, certain that if he turned her over to the sheriff he'd be rid of her. But after that night in the cave, he couldn't. Maddox drew in a deep breath and let it out in a long slow sigh. "I'm not going to turn you over to the sheriff. At least not this one, and not now." He stepped close to her. "However, be warned. I don't like it when people take advantage of me or my family. And I especially don't like it when someone places my family in danger of any kind." He tipped her chin up and stared down into light blue eyes so shiny he could see himself reflected in their depths. "Do you understand?"

She nodded, her bottom lip trembling.

Maddox groaned and kissed her, his mouth crashing down over hers, drawing her into his world and wrapping her in his protection. With her wide, blue eyes, pale skin and diminutive stature, she looked as fragile as a porcelain doll, but her strength and determination to survive shone through.

As quickly as he initiated the kiss, he broke it off, dragging himself several steps away from her. To be that close only rekindled the heat and desire he had no control over. "Join me when you're ready."

As Maddox left the bedroom, his mother met him in the hallway, her hands full of clothing and a hairbrush. "I'll send her along when she's had a chance to change."

A last glance back into the bedroom made Maddox's jaw tighten.

Kat stood with her hands clasped together, the dark circles beneath her eyes making her appear waiflike, vulnerable.

Her presence made him hot, cold, protective and tense all at once. If he had any sense whatsoever, he'd hand her over to the sheriff and save himself and his family the grief she was bound to cause. He turned away, wishing he could wash the image of her staring after him from his mind. Angry that he couldn't, Maddox grabbed a sweatshirt from his own bedroom, tugged it over his head and marched into the living room.

His brother Tuck stood in front of the floor-to-ceiling windows, his back to the view of the snowy-white North Dakota hills. The brightness of the snow behind him cast his brother's face into shadows, consuming his expression and making it completely unreadable.

Maddox almost smiled. Knowing Tuck, he'd done it on purpose to unsettle the sheriff neither of them cared for.

The tall, barrel-chested man standing in the middle of the room turned to greet Maddox, his hand held out. "Maddox."

Maddox hesitated, then took the sheriff's grip. "Sheriff."

The sheriff nodded. "Your brother tells me you rescued a woman out in the canyon."

Maddox nodded. "That's correct." He didn't volunteer any more information than was necessary.

"What was she doing out there?"

"Snowmobiling."

"Damn city people." The sheriff shook his head.

"They've got no sense when it comes to the winters here."

Maddox didn't respond, just stared at the sheriff, willing him to leave.

The sheriff's eyes narrowed as if sizing up Maddox's mood. "Mind if I meet her, see for myself?"

Maddox crossed his arms over his chest. "Why?"

Yost's brows rose. "To see if she's really alive. Come on, a strange woman found in the canyon in a snowstorm isn't an everyday occurrence."

"Any reason to believe she might be dead?" Maddox shot back at him.

The sheriff's eyes narrowed again. "No, none at all. We just get so many missing persons reports over the wire that I like to follow up on them if I get the chance. Has she notified her family of her whereabouts? I'm sure they must be worried by now."

"We'll take care of it," Maddox replied.

Tuck left the shadows and joined Maddox in the middle of the room, facing the sheriff. "Anything else keeping you from performing your civic duties?"

"I'm just paying a friendly visit." His frown deepening, the sheriff glanced down the hallway where Amelia had gone. "If you don't mind, I'll wait and talk to the woman."

Maddox strode to the window and stared out at the stark landscape. Even before the chill of the air closest to the window penetrated his sweatshirt, goose bumps had risen on Maddox's arms. "Why did you come here?"

"I came to see if you and your family—"

"You mean our *mother*," Maddox interrupted.

The sheriff's lips tightened. "—to see if you and your family weathered the storm."

"We're fine. Mother's fine." Tuck took another step closer to the sheriff. "Go find some other family to check on."

Rather than leave, the sheriff sat in John Thunder Horse's favorite chair as if he owned it. "It would be rude of me to leave when *Amelia* asked me to stay."

Maddox wanted to tell him to stay away from his mother, even though he'd been the one insisting that she get out and date again. Date, yes, but not this sheriff, a man his father never trusted.

Sheriff Yost was an arrogant ass and he'd done nothing to find their father's murderer. Getting into a fight with the man would prove nothing and land Maddox in jail.

What good would that do? Where would that leave Kat? Not that she'd be his problem for much longer. As soon as she contacted…whoever, she'd be out of there. "Five minutes with the girl and you leave."

Chapter Five

"I always dreamed of having a girl, but it seemed Mr. Thunder Horse was set on giving me an entire tribe of strapping boys." Amelia bustled about the room, her presence a welcome distraction.

Katya was happy for her company, especially since it meant delaying the inevitable meeting with the sheriff. And the more Maddox's mother talked, the less nervous Katya was.

"I worried all night about Maddox, stuck out there in the cold. I should have known better. He's just like his father—tenacious, industrious and a survivor." She came to stop behind Katya. "Well, almost," she said, her voice catching.

Katya turned in the chair and captured Amelia Thunder Horse's hands in her own, the ache of her own loss still burning in her chest. "What happened to your husband, Mrs. Thunder Horse?"

With a half smile and her eyes suspiciously bright, Amelia recalled the accident that took her husband's life. "He fell off his damned horse." She laughed, the sound more of a sob.

"I'm sorry." A tear slipped from the corner of her eye and Katya squeezed Amelia's hands. "I lost my father recently." She stared up at the older woman. "Does the ache ever go away?"

Maddox's mother smoothed a hand over Katya's temple, tucking a long strand of hair behind her ear. "No. But it does start to subside." Amelia's blue eyes swam with tears of her own.

"I hope it does soon."

"It can take years. It's taken Maddox the past two years to get over the death of his fiancée."

A gasp escaped Katya's lips before she could stop it.

"I don't suppose he told you." The older woman stared at her reflection in the mirror. "They were so much alike, both used to the outdoors, both passionate about the wild horses in the canyon, both born and raised in this desolate part of the country. Such a shame."

Katya looked down at her hands in her lap. How did she compete with someone like that? Not that she was competing. The woman was dead, and Katya wasn't staying around to start anything with the handsome Lakota man who'd saved her life. Her main goal was to stay under the radar of the law and live to find out who'd set her up and who was responsible for her father's murder. Most of the pictures circulating in the media were ones where her hair hung down around her face. Usually an asset, her glossy black locks were a dead giveaway if anyone was looking for her. "I believe I'll pull my hair straight back into a ponytail today."

"But you look so lovely with it down."

"Thank you, but it'll be so much easier to manage up."

"I'll be back in a moment with a rubber band." She left the bedroom.

In seconds, she returned and Katya pulled her hair back into a severe knot.

"Only you could get away with this harsh a hairstyle, my dear."

"How so?"

Amelia tucked a stray hair into the knot. "You have the bearing of royalty."

Her heart skipping a beat, Katya forced a laugh. "My brother would laugh. He thinks I am too much of a hoyden."

"Your brother is so wrong. You're a beautiful young lady. I can see why Maddox is so taken with you."

"Oh, please, Mrs. Thunder Horse. We barely know each other."

"Maybe so, but I know my sons and love them very much. I don't like it when someone tries to hurt any one of them."

Katya's lips twisted. "I understand. I won't be staying long enough for that to happen. Your son has done so much for me already. I'd never hurt him."

"I know you wouldn't—intentionally."

"What do you mean?" Katya thought she'd spent enough time in the United States to understand the nuances of American English. But Amelia's words escaped her comprehension. In the short amount of time she'd known Maddox, she couldn't have had that much of an impact on him, nor he on her. Right?

Last night in the cave, she'd made her own decision and had only one regret—that the night hadn't lasted longer.

"Looks like you're all done." Amelia patted her hair. "I can see why my son saved you."

"He'd have saved me if I'd been a seventy-year-old grandmother."

"You're right. That's Maddox for you, always trying to save the world."

Katya laughed. "I can see that in him."

"His problem is usually that he's so busy saving the world, he doesn't remember to save himself." Amelia laid the brush on the dresser beside the pile of clothing she'd loaned Katya. "Are you feeling okay, dear? Your cheeks are flushed."

The older woman laid a palm across Katya's forehead.

Her face burned hotter at the same time Katya realized how much she missed having a woman care about her. Her own mother had passed away right before Katya's sixteenth birthday. For that brief moment, she closed her eyes and pretended this woman was the mother she missed more than ever. Her eyes burned with unshed tears and a lump rose in her throat. Swallowing hard, she leaned away from Amelia's hand and straightened her shoulders. Wishing didn't make things happen. Both her mother and father weren't coming back. Her brother was missing, her country in turmoil and she was alone in the world. She couldn't bring her family back, but she might be able to help the people of her country. "I'm fine, really."

Amelia stared into her face for a long moment, and sighed. "Come on, then. The men will be wondering what's keeping us."

Katya followed Mrs. Thunder Horse down the hallway to the spacious living room with windows reaching from floor to ceiling and a massive stone hearth blazing with a fire. Despite the warmth of the room, a chill feathered across her skin. Maddox and his brother stood near the window, their backs to the room. A man in a law enforcement uniform sat on the sofa. When he spied Maddox's mother, he rose and extended a hand to her. "Ah, Amelia."

Katya only glanced at the sheriff before her gaze sought out Maddox, the man who had saved her from death and lit a burning fire inside her.

His face could have been made of stone, if not for the muscle twitching in his cheek and the way his fists clenched in tight knots. He didn't even look at her, his gaze pinned on his mother and the man kissing her hand.

"Amelia, my dear," the uniformed man said. "Thank you for seeing me on such short notice."

Amelia blushed and pulled her hand free. "Stop it, William. Please have a seat while I get some hot cocoa. Tuck, why don't you help me?"

Tuck shot a glance at Maddox.

When Maddox didn't look his way, he nudged him in the side.

As if noticing others in the room for the first time, Maddox looked at Katya. "Go on. I can take care of things here," he said to his brother, his voice low.

When Amelia and Tuck left, Katya stood in the middle of the room, alone and completely aware of Maddox's barely leashed anger. She prayed that the sheriff hadn't seen the news or gotten notification to be on the lookout for a suspected terrorist. The only photos the police could have would be those from her apartment, all of which had her hair hanging down, framing her face. Katya hoped that by pulling it back, the sheriff wouldn't recognize her. She fought to keep her nerves steady.

"Five minutes, Yost," Maddox ground out between clenched teeth.

Sheriff Yost raised eyebrows at Maddox and smiled at Katya.

She shivered as if a snail had crawled across her skin, leaving a slimy trail.

"Miss…"

"Evans," Katya finished for him.

"I understand you had a snowmobile accident out in the canyon yesterday."

"That is true."

"Were you with a group?"

"Yes, sir."

"Care to elaborate?"

"It was a tour group out of Bismarck." She prayed she was giving the same answers she'd given Maddox.

"Where is the rest of your group, Miss Evans?"

"I don't know. I lost them." She stared directly at the sheriff, squaring her shoulders. "Is there a reason for all these questions? Am I being arrested or something?"

"No, no." The sheriff held up his hands, smiling, although the smile didn't quite reach his eyes. "I'm just doing my civic duty to protect the good citizens of the county by checking on anything out of the ordinary."

Katya nodded. Fair enough. She just wished this inquisition was over. The longer he was there, the more chance of him recognizing her.

"Three minutes, Yost," Maddox warned.

"Miss Evans, you have an accent." Sheriff Yost crossed the room and walked around her. "Not from around here are you?"

"No." Katya didn't look at the sheriff, her gaze seeking Maddox's, her only rock in this island of uncertainty.

"Foreign?"

"Yes."

"Where from?"

"Russia," she lied. If the police had her passport, they'd know she was from Trejikistan.

"Do you have a visa or passport?"

"Not on me."

"Somewhere you can get to it?"

"If you give me a couple days to send for it." A couple days should allow her enough time to get away from here.

"For a stranger in a foreign country, seems a little odd that you aren't carrying legal documents with you."

"I didn't think I'd need them for a snowmobile ride. I didn't plan on being away for more than a day while I was on the tour." Katya couldn't meet Maddox's gaze as she told one lie after another.

"Is there someone who could forward your documents to you?"

"I hope so."

"So do I. If you can't come up with the necessary proof of legal entry into this country, I'll have to notify Homeland Security."

"I can get you those documents," she insisted, trying to keep her voice calm with no sign of the panic rising like bile in her throat. "I just need time."

The sheriff touched a finger to his chin and tipped his head to the side. "Maybe I should place you in holding until that time comes."

"That won't be necessary." Maddox stepped forward

and slipped an arm around Katya's waist. "She can stay here."

Sheriff Yost's lips pressed into a straight line. "I'll have to check with headquarters. They may want me to secure your little houseguest until she can come up with identification papers."

Katya's heart thundered against her chest. She forced herself to remain composed on the outside. "Completely understandable, Sheriff. If the Thunder Horses are willing to host me until my documents arrive, I would be very happy to stay here." Another lie. Katya fought to keep from choking on the lump rising in her throat.

She had to get word back to Trejikistan and seek out some kind of diplomatic immunity until she could figure out what to do. When she had left Minneapolis, all she had was what she took with her to the church. Her purse, a few credit cards and the remaining U.S. currency she had taken out for incidentals the day before. Her credit cards could be traced, so she cut them in pieces and disposed of them. The little money she had was already gone.

Since she had left the Twin Cities, she had not stopped long enough to call her homeland. She would not know who was left—and who to trust—even when she did.

She could try to get in touch with her cousin, Vladimir Ivanov, on his personal cell phone if he had not also been a target of the takeover. Her personal servants back at the palace were only available through palace telephones and they were not secure. She had to try her cousin when she finally had the chance.

Her passport had been in her apartment, probably confiscated by the police to use as evidence to convict her. She could not stay with the Thunder Horses too long, or the sheriff would begin to get suspicious when her papers failed to arrive. If the sheriff kept up with the news, he might be back sooner with a warrant for her arrest.

No doubt the sheriff would check the databases for anything on Kat Evans. If her pursuer was still trying to track her down—if he didn't think she had died in the snowstorm, he might be listening to police scanners in the area. He might suspect that foreigner, Kat Evans, was really Katya Ivanov and come to check her out for himself.

The sheriff gathered his hat and jacket. His eyes narrowed as he looked across at Katya. "I'll hold Maddox Thunder Horse responsible for your whereabouts until I can review your documents. So don't leave."

"Your five minutes are at an end," Maddox cut in. "And so is my patience."

"Careful, Maddox." Yost glared at Katya's rescuer. "This young lady is a stranger. Who's to say you aren't harboring a criminal?"

Katya gasped, her hand clapping over her lips.

"Get out," Maddox demanded.

"Don't push me."

"Or what? You'll kill me, too?"

"Are you accusing me of something, Thunder Horse?" Yost stood, feet braced, his hands rising dangerously close to his holstered pistol.

Maddox didn't answer, his jaw tight and eyes smoldering.

"Here we are." Amelia sailed into the room, followed by Tuck bearing a large tray filled with steaming mugs.

"Ah, Amelia, how kind." Sheriff Yost smiled and reached for one of the mugs.

Maddox got to it before he did, blocking his path. "The sheriff was just leaving."

"So soon?" His mother pouted, settling the tray on the coffee table.

Yost's smile slipped.

Katya expected him to say something to contradict Maddox. Instead, Yost took Amelia's hands in his. "You're as lovely as ever, Amelia. Much as I'd like to stay, I have work to do. Maybe we can get together for lunch in Medora?"

"No," both Maddox and Tuck said in unison.

Their mother gave them both a stern look before smiling at the sheriff. "That would be nice. How's tomorrow?"

"Perfect." He shot an oily smile at both Maddox and Tucker.

Standing beside Katya, Maddox growled.

Sheriff Yost turned to Katya. "Miss Evans, I'll be in touch. Don't go anywhere until we clear up this matter."

"Yes, sir." Katya vowed to leave as soon as she could. If not to keep her identity safely secret, then to keep the Thunder Horses out of her troubles.

Chapter Six

Maddox's muscles remained tense after Sheriff Yost departed. He walked to the window overlooking the front yard, rolling his shoulders in an attempt to release the pent-up anger over the sheriff's visit.

Sheriff Yost's SUV taillights disappeared down the long drive leading toward the county farm road.

"What did he say?" Tuck stepped up beside Maddox and stood at the window with him.

"You heard him. He wants Kat to stay put until he can contact his superiors or until she can cough up her legal papers."

"We should get Dante in on this. As a member of Customs and Border Protection, he should be up on all the passport regulations."

Katya cringed. Another law enforcement official *and* a member of the family? Great, just what she needed.

Maddox nodded, unaware of the panic rising in Katya. "Isn't he due for a visit?"

"Heard Mom on the phone with him yesterday. He was scheduled to fly over two days ago, but the storm grounded him in Grand Forks."

"The weather's cleared somewhat," Maddox said.

"Right." Tuck turned and strode across the living

room. "I'll call him and see if he's headed this way. If not, at least we can get his take."

"Thanks." Maddox remained at the window, his gaze on the road leading to the homestead. The only indications of the sheriff's visit was the anger burning in Maddox's chest and the tracks left in the newly fallen snow.

Kat crossed the room and stood beside him. "I am sorry. I had no intention of staying or causing you any trouble. I should leave immediately."

"No." The one word came out harsh.

Katya stepped back. "No, what?"

"No, you can't leave." He faced her. "I promised that you would stay here."

Kat's lips tipped upward. "I did not get the impression that you cared for what Sheriff Yost said or did."

"True." Maddox's mouth twitched at the corners and then firmed. "However, for as long as your alien status remains in question, I'm now the responsible party. You stay."

Kat's brows furrowed. Used to bodyguards in her home country, she should have been fine with his determination to protect her. But Maddox wasn't a paid bodyguard. He had been a Good Samaritan in the wrong place at the right time to save her. Now he felt obligated to keep saving her.

Being with her because he wanted to be with her was one thing. Being with her because he was forced into accepting responsibility for her was something entirely different. Kat didn't like it. The more she thought of someone being obligated to watch her like a child, the more the idea grated on the hard-won independence she had been nurturing before her father's death. Staying was not an option. Maddox's stubborn determination to detain her placed her and his family in danger.

What if the man following her tracked her to the Thunder Horse Ranch? Would he attack her here and anyone else who might get in the way?

Then there was the criminal element. If the sheriff matched her face with a wanted poster that might be circulating for a suspected terrorist, the Thunder Horses could be in a lot more trouble for aiding and abetting an alleged dangerous criminal.

Katya closed her eyes and dragged in a deep breath. *Think, Katya, think.* She had to leave. But how could she and not implicate them?

Maddox grabbed her arms. "I don't like that look."

Katya's eyes popped open. "What look?" For a moment she feared he could read her mind and see her plotting her escape. Even more frightening was that he might see the desire ignited by his hold on her arms. His hands squeezed her. Instead of trying to break free, all she could do was recall how his fingers had felt on her naked skin.

"You looked like you were thinking."

She forced a laugh, making light of his comment. "Do not tell me you are one of those men who believe a woman should not have a mind of her own."

"Of course not. But if the woman is dreaming up a cockamamie scheme, I can tell you now, I don't like being surprised." His eyes narrowed. "I'm watching you, so don't do anything we'll both regret."

"Fine," she said. Her brows rose and she stared down at his hands on her arms. "Do you mind?"

He let go as though he hadn't realized he was still

holding her. "What do you need to get your legal documents sent here?"

Katya swallowed her flippant response and settled on, "I need to make a long-distance phone call."

"There's a phone in my office."

"I would rather not impact your long-distance bill." She tipped her head to the side. "Do you have a computer with internet service?"

"Sorry." He shook his head. "We haven't broken down and had the satellite internet service installed yet."

Katya's mouth twisted. "Is there internet service anywhere nearby?"

"Closest is in Medora, a thirty-mile drive."

A surge of hope combined with a sinking in the pit of her belly. "Can you take me there?" She knew what she had to do and it did not make it any easier. If she remembered correctly, Medora was a little town on the interstate highway.

"The library will be closed by now," Maddox said.

Katya had not realized how late it had gotten. At least she had a plan forming. The sooner she executed it, the better. She would contact her homeland via the internet and then hitch a ride as far away from the Thunder Horse Ranch as she could get. Maddox and his family did not need to assume the burden of her problems, nor did they need to be accused as accessories to the crimes someone was trying to frame her for.

"You're doing it again." His hands rose to her arms, only this time he rubbed them gently up and down. "What are you thinking?"

She could not meet his eyes. "How much you and your family have done for me, and how much I appreciate it." She could not tell him goodbye without cluing him in on her plan to escape. At least she could let him know he had done enough. "Thank you." She lifted up on her toes and kissed him.

As soon as her lips touched his, his arms closed around her, drawing her into his embrace. The kiss deepened, his tongue thrusting past her teeth to stroke hers.

Lust and longing burned through her, pressing her body closer. If the kiss could last forever, Katya would be content to let it. Reality had a different plan for her. That plan being to escape and leave Maddox behind. She realized that her plan was only half-baked, as her American classmates would have said. If she wanted to get out of this alive and without spending time in jail, she could not keep running. She had to find out who had set her up. She had to go back to Minneapolis.

A flash of fear streaked through her, making her want to press even closer to Maddox. In the short time she had known him, she had completely relied on his strength and survival skills. Going forward, she would have to do this alone.

Kat broke off the kiss and leaned her forehead against his chest. Their lives were worlds apart. She would have to go home and take on her royal responsibilities, running a country in her father's absence. Until her brother was found alive, she was the next in line for the throne. Katya sighed. As if she didn't have enough to worry about. She backed out of Maddox's reach. "This was never meant to be."

"I know."

Katya's gaze met his, unexpected tears welling in her eyes. She reminded herself that Ivanovs didn't cry.

Before they could spill over and run down her face, she turned away and made a dash for the bedroom she'd shared with Maddox earlier, closing the door between them.

Maddox stared after Kat, his lips tingling, his heart thudding against his rib cage. He hadn't planned on kissing her, but he couldn't help himself. Kissing Kat was as natural as breathing.

The sooner he got her out of his house, off his ranch and out of his life, the sooner he could return to normal.

How he could be drawn to such a woman was beyond him. Susan had been open, honest and straightforward.

Kat had lied to him every step of the way, even down to her name. She was holding back information and he'd better find out what it was before someone got hurt.

Maddox hurried toward the office, intent on calling Pierce, his brother who worked for the FBI, to see if he could dig up anything on Kat Evans or a woman fitting her description. It was a shot in the dark, but a shot worth taking if it led to information on the mysterious woman occupying entirely too much of Maddox's thoughts.

After several rings, his brother answered. "Hello."

"Pierce, Maddox here."

"Hey, brother. How's everything? You guys got hit with a pretty bad storm, didn't you?"

"Yes, we did."

"Have a chance to check on the wild horses to see how they fared?"

"Not yet."

Before Pierce joined the FBI, he'd been just as

involved with tracking the wild horses as Maddox. He always asked, as if they were part of the family. To the Thunder Horses, the horses were a part of their family, their heritage.

"Look, Pierce, I need a favor."

"Name it."

"There's this woman…"

"About time, brother. I know how broke up you were over Susan, but you need to move on. It's been over two years and you aren't getting any younger. I want to be an uncle before I'm too old to enjoy it."

"Pierce, will you shut up for just a minute and let me finish?"

"Don't get your boxers in a wad. Shoot."

"It's not like that." Maddox told him how he'd found Kat and his doubts about her name. "She says she's from Russia—that part I believe. She also said her father recently died. Maybe that will help."

"I'll look into it." Pierce paused then added, "So is she really hot?"

Oh, yeah. With hair the color of midnight, eyes so blue he could fall into them, and a body that, well… "It doesn't matter, she's in some kind of trouble. I need to know what it is before our favorite sheriff finds out."

"Gotcha. She's hot." Pierce laughed. "Give Mom a hug. I'll call as soon as I learn anything."

Maddox hung up and stared out at the sky. Darkness settled in early in the frozen northern states. The clouds had all but disappeared, leaving a crystal-clear blanket of stars scattered across the heavens. Temperatures would drop well below freezing with nothing to keep the warmer air from rising. A chill slithered across Maddox's skin.

He stared out at the night, not seeing any of it, his mind on the stranger in his house. Who was she, and why did she have this power over him?

KAT LAY IN HER BED, dressed in the warm flannel pajamas Mrs. Thunder Horse had loaned her, wishing she were lying naked in a sleeping bag with Maddox.

She sat up, punched her pillow and flopped back down. The man had a way of monopolizing her thoughts when she should be planning her next move. For the next hour she forced herself to think about how she would get word of her survival to her cousin back in Trejikistan. Trying to board an airplane with every Transportation Security Administration staff and police element searching for her would be an impossibility. Even if she managed to board a flight bound for home, there was no way to guarantee her safety upon arrival.

She didn't have a clue what was going on back home. Access to the computer in Medora was imperative—not only to notify her contacts that she was alive, but also to glean anything she could from the news about her country and the power struggle that was surely occurring there. Knowing her cousin, Vladimir, he would have taken temporary control. Which made it all the more important that she return as soon as possible. Vladimir's approach to ruling the small nation was exactly the opposite of her father's vision of a democratic society with free elections.

Surely Vladimir would not have time to force the country to move backward into an autocratic state. All the more reason for her to contact him and let him know she had every intention of returning to rule the country and continue to implement her father's dreams of democracy for Trejikistan.

The more she thought about home, the more her heart ached. Yes, she loved her country and wanted to do right by her people. She could not abandon them to her cousin, Vladimir. Not after her father had made the promise of free elections the next year when they had everything in place and candidates identified. She hoped Vladimir wouldn't resist her claim and declare himself king.

Katya would rather not rule her country. She had been happy that her brother meant to carry on his father's work after he performed a humanitarian mission in Africa. Just two weeks before he was scheduled to return, his convoy had been ambushed. Some of his team were killed, but they never found her brother's body. Her father had been devastated, and Katya was preparing to go back to Trejikistan when she had received word that her father had been in an accident as well.

Her mind roiled with all that happened in the past couple of weeks, her heart heavy for her losses. As the hours passed and the night wore on, exhaustion claimed her.

A sound jerked her awake. Or at least she thought it was a sound. She might have been dreaming, but she could not slow the thump of her heart against her chest. Katya's eyes opened wide and she looked around the room. Starlight shone through the gap in the curtain, allowing a narrow blue ray across the room. From her vantage point, nothing moved.

Having been followed and shot at, Katya was not leaving anything to chance. She rolled over in the bed and eased herself to the floor, using the bed as cover and concealment. If someone was in the room, she did not have much of a chance. If the noise was from outside the house, she needed to hide until the source was discovered.

After several long minutes, she ventured to the end of the bed, her gaze darting from the window to the door that connected her room to Maddox's. Should she check out the noise herself or wake Maddox and have him check it out?

Calling herself a coward, Katya chose to alert Maddox. If she investigated the strange sound alone, she had no backup, no way to alert the rest of the family should something happen to her.

Keeping low to the ground, with the bed between her and the window, she crept toward the door. As she reached for the knob, another sound penetrated the thrum of blood banging against her eardrums. Her flight instincts kicked in, she twisted the knob and dove into the room.

"What the hell?" Maddox leaped from the bed and landed in a crouched stance, his fists clenched. He stared down at her, his eyes narrowing. "Kat?"

"Shh…" She pressed a finger to her lips. "I heard something outside."

Maddox grabbed her and pulled her around to the other side of his massive bed. "Stay here."

"No. I can check on it. I just wanted you to know." She tried to get up, but he held her down.

"I know this house better than you do. Promise me you'll stay put." He waited, refusing to move until she complied.

"I promise." She did not like hiding behind the bed when Maddox might be placing himself in danger.

Instead of going to the window, he tiptoed out into the hallway. He moved so stealthily, Katya couldn't tell which way he had gone.

All she knew was that he could be in danger, and it was all because of her.

Several long minutes passed. Katya could not hear or see anything from where she sat, and the suspense was making her crazy with worry. When she could not stand it any longer, she crept out into the hallway.

A light sprang to life in the living area and low male voices rumbled, one of them belonging to Maddox.

Katya hurried toward the sound. When she emerged into the light, Maddox and Tuck looked at her.

"You promised."

"I did stay for as long as I could. What was the sound?"

Tuck stared at her. "Someone was prowling around outside the house."

Maddox crossed his arms over his chest. "Care to enlighten us on who it might be?"

Katya's eyes widened, her cheeks burning. "How would I know? I did not go outside." What was it the Americans said? The best defense was a good offense. She hoped that was the case. She could use a good defense with Maddox glaring down at her.

How could she talk her way out of this one? She had to get to Medora tomorrow before she could escape the Thunder Horse clan. They didn't need to know any more than they already did. The more they knew the more likely they'd be arrested for helping her.

Maddox shook his head. "Not buying it. Try the truth."

Chapter Seven

Maddox waited, anger burning inside.

The way Kat's gaze darted from Tuck and back to him didn't give him any confidence that she would tell the truth this time.

"Really." She sighed and stared at her feet. "I do not know who it was."

Anger exploded in him and Maddox grabbed her arms. "No more lies. I want the truth."

She stared up at him, her eyes an icy-blue, glistening with unshed tears. "I am telling you the truth. I do not know who is after me."

Tuck laid a hand on his shoulder. "Let her go, Maddox."

He ignored his brother, shaking his hand off. "I saved your life in that snowstorm, and you repay me by feeding me lie after lie."

"I am deeply sorry." Her gaze dropped to where his hands rested on her arms, squeezing hard. "I have no idea who was outside my window."

"You said you didn't know who was after you."

Kat stilled, refusing to look up from her feet.

"Is that why you were in the canyon? Someone was after you?"

She squared her shoulders and looked across the room, her gaze never making contact with him. "I got lost and fell into the canyon."

Maddox didn't move and didn't say anything. He'd been having romantic thoughts about this woman, something he hadn't done since Susan's death. She'd been lying to him, and he'd been stupid, knowing she lied and not caring.

He cared now. When it came to endangering his family, he didn't take kindly to a stranger's lies.

"Look, whoever it was is gone. Let's get some sleep." Tuck plucked Kat from Maddox's grip. "I'll stand watch over our guest." He turned to lead her away.

Maddox, unwilling to let go of his anger so easily, removed Tuck's hand from around Kat's waist, but didn't replace it with his own "I found her, I'm the one answering to Yost for her. I'll keep watch."

"You get all the fun stuff." Tuck shrugged. "Have it your way. I'm going to bed."

Kat didn't wait for them to settle the argument. She headed for her room.

Maddox let her go, entering his own room. Once inside, Maddox paced the floor. He hated it when he was lied to. Even worse, he hated when he still felt protective of the one who'd lied. How could she stand there and refuse to tell him the truth, yet still look like the victim?

And what kind of fool was he to continue to play her game? Anger pushed him through the door and into the connecting room.

Kat lay in the bed, the coverlet pulled up to her chin, her ice-blue eyes wide and wary. "What do you want?"

"The truth."

"I've told you the truth. I can't help that you don't believe me."

"You aren't telling me everything."

"I've told you what I can."

He stared at her. Even with the sheet pulled up to her chin, wearing those ridiculous flannel pajamas his mother had given her, she looked sexy.

He strode across the room and flung the blanket back.

Kat yelped and drew her knees up to her chest.

"You're coming with me." Grabbing her hand, he pulled her up and led her to his room.

She yanked her hand free and backed away from the king-sized bed. "I cannot sleep with you."

"Why not? It's not as if you haven't already."

"I know." She twisted a button on the pajama top and backed up another step. "I just can't."

"It's too late to go modest on me. Get in the bed."

"No."

Maddox scooped her in his arms and deposited her in the middle of the mattress. "You're staying where I can keep an eye on you."

She scooted across the bed to the farthest corner, glaring at him. "Barbarian."

"Keep it up, and I'll show you barbarian." He stripped his sweatpants and sweatshirt off and crawled into the bed in his boxer shorts. He rolled over to switch the light off. "I suggest you sleep. And don't try anything."

"Why? Are you going to throw me again?"

"No, but I'm about ready to turn you over to the sheriff."

She sat at the foot of the bed, her arms wrapped

around her flannel-clad knees, her eyes wide, glowing in the starlight streaming in through the window. "You would do that?"

"You haven't given me any reason not to."

"Would it help if I told you it is for your own good?"

"No." He turned away, afraid that if he continued to stare at her, he'd do something stupid, like take her in his arms and make love to her. "I suspect you're in a whole lot of trouble and we've only just scratched the surface."

His body ached with the desire he fought to control. Those damn pajamas had a stronger impact on him than seeing her naked.

Kat sat for a while at the end of the bed.

Maddox feigned sleep.

Eventually, she crawled beneath the covers, keeping as far away from him as possible.

He knew she was there. His body recognized every movement. Her scent filled the air and drove him crazy with need.

Tomorrow he had to do something to get her out of his life.

KAT WOKE TO THE SUN streaming through the window, and the other side of the bed empty. She'd done something she hadn't done in a long time. She had silently cried herself to sleep. She sat up and stared across the room into the mirror hanging over the dresser.

Her hair stood on end, the masses of curls a riotous mess. Her blotchy skin and red-rimmed eyes did nothing to instill a sense of confidence in her.

The door to the bedroom opened, and Mrs. Thunder Horse entered, bearing a tray loaded with food. "Good morning." She smiled brightly and laid the tray on the dresser. "I figured that after all the fuss last night, you'd be too tired to join us at the breakfast table."

"Really, Mrs. Thunder Horse, you are not my servant. I could have come to the table."

"I rarely have guests. Please, let me spoil you a little."

"But I am not a guest. I am just one who has been foisted upon you and your family."

"In my view, that makes you a guest, and this is my chance to pull out the good china. I can't believe I slept through everything last night."

"I'm sorry there was such a fuss."

"Why should you be sorry? It's not as though you invited whoever it was to lurk around outside our house."

"Your son seems to think I did. Or at least that I invite trouble."

"Maddox tends to see only the black and white. Gray disturbs him. It's out of his control and he's uncomfortable with things he can't control."

Katya smiled at the woman. "You remind me of my mother. Thank you."

Amelia's cheeks reddened. "Oh, well then. You're quite welcome. How about some food?"

What Katya wanted most was to know where Maddox was, but she did not want to sound anxious or needy. Not when she planned to escape Maddox's protective custody as soon as the opportunity presented itself.

"Maddox is out helping Tuck feed the animals. He said to be ready when he gets back in. He'll run you to town."

And drop her off at the sheriff's office? A shiver

of apprehension feathered across the back of her neck. Sheriff Yost would lock her up so tight, she would never see the light of day if he knew she was a suspected terrorist. The sooner she left the county, the better off she and the Thunder Horses would be. "Do you have a pen and paper I could use?"

"Certainly." Amelia laid the tray on the bed. "I didn't know what you eat in Russia or what you like to eat in America, so I put a little of everything on your plate."

"I could not possibly eat all of that."

"I don't expect you to. Enjoy. I'll be back with your pen and paper." Amelia sailed out of the room.

Katya picked at the toast and scrambled eggs, her appetite less than healthy. The thought of leaving Maddox did not inspire her to eat. Yet she knew if she wanted to find the man who framed her, she would have to keep her strength up. With that in mind, she forced herself to finish the food and she downed the glass of orange juice.

By the time Amelia returned, she had finished eating and gotten out of bed to dress.

"Here are your clothes, dear. Now, I've got to go finish my grocery list for Maddox to pick up while you two are in town." She paused at the door. "How does baked chicken sound for supper?"

Kat almost cried again. She hated to disappoint the woman, but she had no intention of returning. "Baked chicken sounds wonderful."

Mrs. Thunder Horse beamed. "Good." The older woman left the room, a spring in her step.

She'd be making food for a guest who would not be there if Katya's plans worked out the way she hoped. She quickly dressed in the clothing Amelia had thoughtfully cleaned and returned to her room. Someday she hoped she could return all the favors this family had bestowed upon her during her stay. But for now, survival and proving her innocence took precedence.

She was just zipping her snow boots when Maddox arrived, filling the doorway.

"Ready?"

"I am." She stood, straightening her shoulders.

He didn't say anything, just turned and walked down the hallway.

Katya assumed she was to follow.

Amelia gave Maddox her list and hugged him before he pushed through the door.

She surprised Katya with an equally warm hug, which threatened to bring more tears to her eyes.

A blast of cold wind swirled in, enveloping Katya in its icy clutches. She had not been out in the cold since they'd come in from the storm. The wind chill bit into her exposed skin, sending violent shivers across her entire body. She hurried down the steps and out into the snow-covered drive where Maddox stood next to a large truck with knobby tires.

She rounded the hood to the passenger side and climbed up into the truck. The interior of the truck smelled of hay and leather. The gloves on the seat beside her explained the scent of leather. Beside it was a handheld radio.

Maddox climbed into the driver's seat and started the engine.

Tuck came down the steps of the house with a paper in his hand. "You forgot Mom's list. And I just heard from Dante. He's on his way and will be here in less than an hour."

"Good. Let him know we've headed into town. We'll see him when we get back." Maddox took the list and hit the button to close the power window and block out the blasts of cold wind filling the truck.

Katya huddled in the seat, quietly taking it all in and trying to be as invisible as she could be in the tight confines of the pickup truck.

They made the thirty-mile drive in just under an hour on the snowy roads.

When they arrived in Medora, Maddox parked in the library parking lot and got out.

"I can do this myself," Katya insisted.

"Without a driver's license, they might not let you use the internet." Maddox's dark brows rose. "Got one of those?"

"No."

Maddox led the way into the facility and proceeded to charm the librarian into letting Katya use a computer with internet access without a driver's license or passport.

As she sat in front of the computer screen, Katya wondered how she could tell Maddox to go away so that she could send her message in secrecy. He had been right to be angry with her last night. After saving her life, he should expect her to be forthcoming with the facts. But she did not want him to know anything in case the authorities interrogated him and his family. She had to have time to discover the real culprit.

Just when she opened her mouth to tell Maddox to go get the groceries his mother wanted, a cell phone rang in Maddox's pocket.

Katya jumped. "They get reception out here?"

His lips twisted into a grimace. "Sometimes." He dug

in his pocket and pulled out the phone. "Excuse me." Maddox walked toward the front entrance to the library and out into the street, speaking into the receiver.

Katya breathed a sigh of relief and hoped whoever it was would stay on the line long enough for her to get word to her people. She had spied a gas station not far from the library. A large tractor-trailer rig had been parked there, the driver filling the tank. If she hurried, she might be able to catch a ride with him, assuming he was headed for Minneapolis.

She keyed in the web address of her internet provider and brought up her email. Several of the students in her master's program had sent emails asking her where she was, and when she would have her portion of their group project done. A stab of guilt made her skip past them quickly and click on an email from her former bodyguard.

If she trusted anyone, it was Andrei Sokolov. He had protected her for most of her childhood. Since she had been gone, he had been in a state of semi-retirement, augmenting the team of bodyguards protecting her father. She had been in contact with him, exchanging emails like old friends up until two days ago. The message was short and in her native Russian. "Where are you?"

She quickly typed, "Are you there now?" Katya hit the Send button and glanced over her shoulder toward the glass front door of the library. Maddox stood with his back to her, the cell phone pressed to his ear, hunching his back against the wind.

Please be there, Andrei, please. She rubbed her fingers over the pendant her father had given her, wishing her friend would come online. She needed to communicate with someone from home.

It would be close to nine o'clock in the evening in Trejikistan. Andrei liked to go online and send emails at that time. Hopefully, the turmoil in the country had not changed that. After several long seconds, Katya realized that she'd never have time to wait for his response and still catch a ride with the trucker. She composed a brief message to let Andrei know that she was okay and that she had trouble in the States. She would contact him when she had more information and let her cousin know that she would return to Trejikistan as soon as possible.

She signed off the email, erased the computer's history and shut it down.

Katya stole a glance at the door where Maddox still stood with his back to her. Pulling the paper and pen Amelia had given her from her pocket, she dashed off a quick note of thanks to Maddox and folded the paper. She hurried to the front desk and asked the librarian to give it to Maddox when he came back in.

Then pretending that she needed to use the ladies' room, she walked toward the narrow hallway where the bathrooms were located as well as the rear exit door.

Before she could change her mind, she slipped through the back exit and out into the open. Katya hurried toward the corner of the building and peered around. The space between the library and the next building was empty. She ducked behind the next building and ran to the end. A gust of wind whipped her red scarf up into her face. Temporarily blinded by the scarf, she did not see the person behind her until too late. A gloved hand clamped over her mouth and another lifted her off her feet and ran her toward the open trunk of a car waiting in the gap between the buildings.

Kat kicked and tried to scream, but the wind carried away what little sound made it through the thick gloves. She braced her feet on the car, refusing to let the man shove her inside. Once in, she knew her chances of escaping were slim to none.

The man kicked at the backs of her knees and her legs buckled enough for him to shove her through the opening, slamming the trunk lid over her.

Darkness and the smell of tire rubber and exhaust surrounded her, filling Katya with despair.

Chapter Eight

"Yes, she has black hair and ice-blue eyes," Maddox said into the cell phone, having a hard time hearing his brother, Pierce, over the wail of the wind.

"Pretty?"

"We established that the last time we talked."

"I think you have a problem on your hands, my man."

"Tell me what I don't know." Maddox shifted the phone to the other ear. "What did you find out?"

"One Katya Ivanov, a college student, from a Russian breakaway country called Trejikistan, went missing from her apartment here in Minneapolis two days ago."

"Katya." She hadn't been lying about that part of her name and Ivanov was close to Evans. "So? Why the fuss?"

"Her picture is all over the news in Minnesota, and CNN picked up on it today."

Maddox gripped the phone hard. "What the hell did she do?"

"Bad news, brother."

As if what he'd already learned wasn't bad enough. He steeled himself for more. "What?"

"Authorities suspect her of plotting a terrorist attack based on the weapons and explosives they found in her closet. They have flyers going out to all the law enforcement agencies in Minnesota and all the surrounding states. They want to bring her in for questioning. I have my people digging into her background."

Maddox let out a long breath. "Wow. I guess that's why she didn't want to tell me anything." He shook his head, calling himself every kind of fool. "Great. I was harboring a potential terrorist."

"Not a good place to be, bro. You know I'll have to report it."

"Do that. It's what I get for saving a stranger's life."

"You can't blame yourself. You didn't know."

Maddox snorted. "I knew she was lying."

"But you didn't know about what."

Still, he hadn't followed that gut feeling, instead following lust.

"You have to bring her in."

"Where?" Maddox kept his back to the library, afraid Katya would suspect him of plotting to turn her in. "I can't turn her over to the sheriff. Yost is a sadistic bastard. He'd use this to hurt her and our family."

"If you could keep her away from Yost for the day, I could be there to take her off your hands. I have a buddy with a private pilot's license. He could get me there in as little as five hours."

"Let's do it. She already has someone following her. I'm not sure who it is, but I suspect he chased her into the canyon. I don't know how dangerous he is. You might check and see if it's one of your guys."

"Will do. I'm on my way as soon as I can secure a plane ride. Keep her close."

"Right." Maddox hit the End button, terminating the call. What was Katya doing on the internet? Sending notes to her terrorist buddies? Maddox pushed through the door and hurried across the floor.

"Sir?" As Maddox passed by the front desk, the librarian held out a folded piece of paper. "The young lady you came in with asked me to give you this."

He grabbed the paper, jammed it into his pocket and kept on walking toward the bank of computers. The seat where he'd left Kat was empty, the computer screen blank.

Great, just great. She'd ducked out on him. Maddox ran through the shelves of books, searching for a backdoor, finding it in the aisle with the bathrooms. She had to have gone out this way. She hadn't come through the front.

As he ran out the back, he looked left then right. A man struggled at the back of a dark blue car and finally slammed the trunk. Before the lid closed, Maddox could see a flash of red scarf and coal-black curly hair. He heard a female cry for help.

"Kat!" Maddox ran toward the car.

The man jumped into the driver's seat before Maddox could get close enough to stop him.

The car pulled away as Maddox reached it, only giving him enough time to slam his hand against the metal doorframe before the vehicle skidded out into the street and headed south out of town.

Maddox yanked his cell phone from his pocket and punched in the number for Dante. He didn't wait for an answer, sprinting out onto the main road and back to the library where his truck was parked. Dante's number went directly to an answering machine. Damn reception!

He tried his house. Maybe Dante had already arrived there.

After the second ring, Dante answered. "I just landed at the ranch. Where are you and your hot foreign number?"

"Crank up your bird and get over to Medora ASAP!"

"What's going on?"

"Someone just snatched Kat. They're headed south out of town in a dark blue, four-door sedan."

"How do you know he snatched her and she didn't go willingly?"

Maddox climbed in behind the wheel of his truck, flipped the ignition and yanked the gearshift into reverse. "She was thrown in the trunk. Can you hurry? And bring the handheld radio. Cell reception is nil once you leave town."

"On it. I'll bring Tuck with me. We'll see you in a few."

Maddox flung the phone onto the seat next to him and slammed his foot down on the accelerator. The truck shot forward, the back end fishtailing on the ice.

By the time Maddox had his truck on the road, the car carrying Kat was long gone. He hoped and prayed that the kidnapper didn't turn off the main highway onto one of the side roads.

Kat must have slipped out the backdoor of the library and run into trouble outside. Her attacker couldn't have grabbed her from inside the building without raising a ruckus and alerting the library staff.

Maddox pounded his palm against the steering wheel. How had he let this happen? He'd only been away from her for a few minutes, talking to his brother. Hell, why did he even care?

Kat hadn't planned on sticking around. That had to be why she'd convinced him to come to town. To make contact with her people.

Really. Why did he care? She'd lied to him, tried to ditch him and could be a terrorist. Why was he so concerned that someone had kidnapped her?

An image of her lying naked in his arms, the soft glow of the flashlight shining in her eyes and on her hair came to mind. His groin tightened and his foot pressed the gas pedal to the floor.

She'd reawakened him, reminding him what it was like to allow himself to care again. The least she could do was live long enough to tell him the truth. Had making love to him been a means to an end? Had she only given herself to sucker him into protecting her?

Kat had dragged Maddox from the fog of the emotionless existence he'd buried himself in for the past two years. An existence in which he refused to care about anyone who wasn't family. Maddox now warred with the full spectrum of emotions. Anger, betrayal, fear and... *oh, please, no*...the potential to love again.

Hadn't he been better off emotion-free?

Ten miles outside Medora, Maddox worried that he'd gone in the wrong direction. He hadn't seen the car, even on the long, straight, flat stretches of road. Had the kidnapper gotten that far ahead or had he taken a side road Maddox missed?

Overhead the loud rumble of an aircraft engine and the telltale thumping of rotary blades made Maddox let out the breath he held. The green-and-white CBP helicopter blew past him, following the ribbon of highway.

Several miles ahead, the helicopter slowed and appeared to be hovering or moving very slowly.

The handheld radio buzzed on the seat next to him. He grabbed it and hit the Talk button.

"Hey, it's Tuck. We just passed you and found a dark blue four-door car ahead on the highway." The radio crackled, static blasting in his ear, but Maddox held onto it like a lifeline.

"That's it," he shouted.

"Two miles ahead over the next rise. He's going pretty fast."

"Can you slow him down or stop him?"

"How? You want Dante to land on him? He's already in enough trouble taking the chopper out on non–Border Patrol business."

"Never mind." Maddox pushed his truck past the safe driving speed for icy roads. "Just keep him in sight until I catch up."

"Then what? If we force him off the road, he might crash." The static increased, filling Maddox's ear.

Maddox's chest tightened. No matter how many lies Kat had told him, she didn't deserve to be kidnapped or to die in the trunk of a car.

"We'll figure it out when I get closer." Maddox stuffed the radio into his pocket. As his truck closed in on the helicopter's position, the dark blue sedan came into view.

The man drove like a lunatic with a death wish, spewing snow and ice behind his tires. He slowed and turned off the main road into an area Maddox knew to be filled with ravines and canyons dropping off the sides of the road. If they didn't stop him soon, he could easily slip off the road and crash down a sheer drop.

Dante's helicopter dipped low over the car as Maddox caught up.

The car hit a bump of ice on the poorly maintained road. The wheels jerked to the right, launching the car up a ramp of snow, pitching it over the edge of the road and down into a steep ravine.

Maddox's heart skipped several beats before kicking into an adrenaline-pumping machine. He forced himself to slow gradually on the snow and ice until he could come to a complete and safe halt at the point where the car disappeared off the edge of the road.

Slamming the gearshift into Park, Maddox dropped down out of the truck and ran to the road's edge. Far below in the bottom of a deep crevice, the sedan lay on the passenger side, its front wheels still spinning.

Panic threatened to paralyze Maddox. He pictured Susan lying lifeless in his arms. He couldn't and wouldn't let that happen to Kat. He leaped over the edge and scrambled down the hill toward the mangled vehicle, his breath hung in his throat, his legs shaky and threatening to buckle with each step.

She couldn't be dead. Not Kat. She had too much determination to survive.

A shot rang out, the bullet pinging off the rocks next to Maddox's feet. He threw himself behind a large out-cropping of boulders, knowing the trip down the ravine made him an ideal target for someone below. More shots hit the rocks and dirt behind him.

He glanced toward the sky. As if on cue, the helicopter flew over with Tuck leaning out the door, a rifle in his hand, firing at the kidnapper.

The overwhelming rumble of the helicopter was all that Maddox could hear. Soon the chopper eased farther away, following the flow of the ravine down into a small canyon.

With the helicopter noise gone, the sounds of gunfire had ceased. Maddox couldn't see a shooter. He had to assume Tuck's cover fire had chased him off.

Kat could be injured in the trunk, maybe bleeding.

Unable to wait a moment longer, Maddox abandoned the relative safety of the boulder and continued his descent.

As though moving in slow motion, he slipped and slid on snow, ice and rocks, until he landed beside the vehicle.

With the car lying on its side, the undercarriage facing him, Maddox couldn't see inside. No one had shot at him on his trek down the hill, but that didn't mean the guy wasn't hiding, waiting for his chance to nail an easy target.

Maddox eased up the undercarriage of the overturned vehicle and peered down into the interior. Nothing moved. The driver's window was gone, shards of glass scattered all over the seats.

"Kat!" Maddox said, loudly enough so she could hear him, but hopefully not so loud that the shooter could zero in on him.

"Maddox?" Kat's muffled voice sounded from the rear of the vehicle. "I cannot get out. Find the key."

Still up on the side of the car, Maddox felt around the steering column until he found the keys. He yanked them from the ignition, pushed backward and dropped to the ground, glancing around for signs of the shooter.

When he moved around to the back of the car, he

groaned. The trunk lay wedged against a huge boulder. Even with the key, he couldn't get the trunk open.

"Hang on, Kat. I'm going to need more help."

"Hurry!"

Maddox pulled the handheld radio from his pocket and hit the Talk button, praying the helicopter was in range. "Where are you guys?"

"Following your sedan driver. He disappeared into the canyon."

"Leave him. I need your help here." Maddox explained the position of the car and what he needed to get Kat out.

The helicopter rumbled into sight and hovered over Maddox.

Tuck appeared in the door, leaned out and latched a cable to the skid, dropping the coil of cable down below the helicopter.

Dante eased the helicopter above where Maddox stood, the cable dangling closer and closer until Maddox could grab the hook and direct it toward the undercarriage.

He hooked the cable on the car and waved up at Dante.

Tuck, rifle in hand, scanned the terrain below the helicopter.

Maddox climbed up the hill and to one side of where the car rested. "Hang on, Kat! The ride's going to get bumpy again."

Maddox waved to Tuck. Tuck leaned into the helicopter.

The cable tightened, the helicopter straining against the weight of the vehicle.

Maddox held his breath, hoping that by righting the car it wouldn't slip farther down the ravine.

Metal scraped and groaned and the car teetered, swaying toward the helicopter. Gravity kicked in and the car dropped toward the ground, tugging hard on the cable.

The helicopter dropped a couple feet before it steadied and hovered low enough for the cable to hang loosely.

Maddox unhooked the cable from the undercarriage of the car and waved at Tuck who gathered his end and reeled the cable back up into the chopper.

The helicopter lifted higher into the sky and circled back toward where the attacker had disappeared.

"Kat?" Maddox slipped and slid down the rocky hillside to the back of the car and stopped.

"Surprisingly, I am still here," she said through the metal of the trunk.

Maddox fitted the key in the lock and twisted. Dented and battered, the lid didn't budge. He fit his fingers beneath the edges and lifted hard, throwing his back into freeing Kat.

Metal scraped against metal and the trunk sprang open.

Kat blinked up at him, her face bruised, her hair tangled and matted with blood from a gash on her forehead, but she was as beautiful as ever.

Maddox reached for her, pulling her out of the trunk and into his arms.

Kat clung to him, her body shaking, speaking in a language he couldn't understand, her words coming fast and furious.

He tipped her face up to his and stared down into icy-blue eyes awash in tears. Then his mouth crashed down over hers with the force of his anger, his desperation and his fear. He couldn't stop the flood of emotion he experienced whenever he was around her, and he hated himself for his lack of control.

Her hands circled behind his neck and if it was possible, she drew him closer, kissing him back as if they were the last man and woman on earth.

When he came up for air, Maddox pushed aside the intense relief and allowed his anger to resurface. "When we get back to the ranch, you're going to tell me everything. Do you understand? Especially what the hell you were planning to do with the guns and explosives."

Chapter Nine

Katya sat in a straight-backed chair in the Thunder Horse living room as Amelia cleaned the blood off her forehead using a damp cloth. Tumbling down a hill in the trunk of a car had taken its toll on her and she had the lumps and bruises to show for it.

As Amelia worked her magic, Maddox paced the floor in front of her, finally coming to a halt. "That's good, Mom. She can do the rest later."

Amelia Thunder Horse shot a narrow-eyed glare at her son. "Don't you think she's been through enough?"

Maddox crossed his arms over his chest and shook his head, his lips pressed into a thin line. "We haven't even begun."

Undeterred, Maddox's mother dabbed antibiotic ointment on the gash, plastered a bandage over it and stepped back. "She could have a concussion. She really needs to see a doctor."

Katya shook her head, a blast of fear racing through her veins. "No."

Maddox's mouth twisted. "Care to tell my mother why you don't want to see a doctor?"

The harshness of Maddox's gaze sent a chilling wash of despair over Katya, making her feel colder than if she'd been lying beside the river in a bank of snow. For a brief moment she'd allowed herself to rely on Maddox to protect her. But that was over. She squared her shoulders and lifted her chin the way her father taught her when facing her adversaries. "What do you know?"

"That you've been lying to us all along. Your name is Katya Ivanov, you were a student in Minneapolis and you're a terrorist."

Amelia gasped. "Maddox!"

"What?" Maddox pinned Katya with his stare. "It's true, isn't it?"

Katya winced, at once relieved and concerned that he still didn't know the whole picture. What he did know was bad enough. She drew in a deep breath and let it out. "Part of what you just said is true."

Maddox's eyes blazed and he stalked across the wood floor to stand in front of her, trapping her in the chair. He leaned over her, bracing his hands on the chair's arms. "The part about lying to us? Or the part about being a terrorist?"

Katya leaned back in order to look directly up into Maddox's eyes. She held his gaze, determined to give as good as she got. All the while her heart pounded in her chest, her breath catching in her throat at his nearness. "My name and the part about being a student in Minneapolis."

"What are you talking about, Maddox?" Amelia touched her son's arm. "Katya isn't a terrorist."

"Evidence indicates otherwise." He directed his words at Katya. "Doesn't it?"

Anger bubbled up inside Katya. She had been through hell and she was damn tired of it. "Not everything is as it appears. And if you would give me a chance, I will explain."

"You've had more chances than I can count to explain yourself, to tell the truth, but you didn't."

"I did not want to get you and your family involved in my troubles."

"Hate to tell you, darlin', but we already are." Maddox pushed away from the chair and towered over her. "Since we're about as deeply involved as we can get by harboring a terrorist, maybe you can enlighten us."

Katya stood, placing herself toe-to-toe with Maddox. "I came to the United States to go to school, not to blow it up. The weapons they found in my apartment are not mine. Someone set me up. You have to believe me."

"Why? You've lied to me from the beginning."

"I had to." She looked around the room at the faces of Maddox's family. "When I woke up in that cave, I did not know who you were. I do not know who has been following me or why, but he tried to kill me."

"And you thought I might be him?"

Katya shrugged. "I didn't know. I was unconscious when you found me."

"So you slept with the enemy, just in case?"

Katya's face burned, anger making her pulse race with the need to strike back. Dammit, she was the victim, not the villain. "That is correct. Keep your friends close and your enemies closer." She turned to the others in the room, avoiding Maddox. "I am not a monster bent on destroying your country. I am a student who has been targeted by someone, for what reason I do not know." She had her suspicions, but she was not sharing them until she knew for certain. "Go back to the canyon and find the snowmobile. You will see the proof."

"Proof that I was a fool to believe you in the first place?" Maddox ground out, no pity in his gaze for the woman he'd rescued.

Katya swayed, her head throbbing. "Proof that whoever is after me is shooting real bullets."

Amelia gasped, hurrying over to Katya. "Maddox, you've bullied her enough. Let the child lie down. She's been shot at, almost frozen to death and now she's been in a car wreck. I'm surprised she's still on her feet."

"She still hasn't told us why the weapons were in her apartment." His brows rose. "Why—Kat—Katya or whoever you are?"

"I do not know! I am a student and a citizen of Trejikistan, not a terrorist."

Maddox crossed his arms over his chest, his jaw taut, but for a muscle twitching in the side. "Give me one reason why I shouldn't turn you over to the authorities right now?"

"I'll give you one." Tuck grinned. "Yost is the only *authority* in the neighborhood. I wouldn't turn over a rabid dog to that man."

"Tuck!" Amelia admonished. "Sheriff Yost is an officer of the law."

Tuck snorted. "Maybe he should pay more attention to the law."

"Turning her over to Yost will only make it bad on you, Maddox," Maddox's brother, Dante, said. "He won't wait to get the truth."

Tuck shook his head. "The man wouldn't know the truth if it bit him in the—"

"Tuck!" Amelia planted her hands on her hips. "What would your father say?"

Maddox's gaze shifted from Katya to his mother,

his expression softening. "A lot more if he were still here."

"But he's not. And we have to carry on." Amelia sighed. "Why are you all so down on Sheriff Yost? He's been nothing but good to me since your father's death."

Tuck crossed to his mother and draped an arm over her shoulders. "We don't trust him, Mom." When she opened her mouth to argue, Tuck held up a hand. "Don't ask why, we just don't."

Dante stood. "Which comes back to our little problem here."

Katya's lips twisted into a grimace. "By *problem*, I assume you mean me."

Maddox nodded, the frown a permanent fixture on his forehead since they'd returned to the Thunder Horse Ranch.

She sighed, her shoulders drooping with the weight of fatigue and defeat. "I did not put those weapons in my apartment. Someone else did. And I do not know why."

Dante stood with his arms crossed over his chest. "The question is what to do with her until we have an answer. I could turn her in to Customs and Border Patrol as an illegal alien."

Maddox didn't respond.

Katya held her breath. If they turned her over to the police or CBP, she might never learn the truth and be punished for a crime she had not committed.

Tuck moved to the window and peered out. "You'd better figure out the solution quick. Our favorite sheriff just drove up."

"He's here to take me to lunch." Amelia hurried

toward the door. "Relax. I'll take care of the sheriff. Maddox, you take care of Katya. Go out the back, I'll keep him inside long enough for you both to escape."

While Amelia hurried toward the door, Maddox stared across at Kat. "What's it going to be? Come with me, go with the Border Patrol or go with the sheriff?"

She shrugged. "You have to do what you feel is right. If you are so certain that I am a terrorist, you should turn me over to the law. If it makes it any easier, I'll go now." She took two steps in the direction Amelia had gone before Maddox blocked her path.

"No." He pushed his hand through his long hair and sighed. "I don't know who you are or what your game is, but for now, you'll come with me."

"Where?" she demanded.

"I don't know. But you're my problem until I can figure this mess out. Get your coat and gloves. It'll be cold outside."

Railroaded into agreeing, Katya went for her outdoor gear, gathering her coat, gloves and scarf while Maddox spoke quietly with his brothers.

Katya could hear his mother talking to the sheriff and the sheriff's answering murmur. Her pulse quickened, fear pushing her forward despite how tired she was and how much her head hurt.

When she emerged from the bedroom, Maddox met her, outfitted in a heavy winter coat, carrying gloves and a bag. He marched Katya through the house, urging her to silence with a finger pressed to his lips.

At the backdoor, she paused. "I'm sorry I brought you and your family into this."

"No more so than I am." He held the door open and a blast of frigid air blew in.

Katya shrugged into her coat and gloves and stepped out onto the porch. "If you could get me to the interstate, I could leave you and your family in peace."

"You're not going anywhere until we figure out exactly what trouble you're in."

"But you don't have to help me." She stared up into his eyes.

"I'm not. I'm helping myself and my family." His lips thinned into a tight line and he gazed down at her. "If you are a terrorist, we are all guilty of harboring you. I don't plan on my family going to jail because I was fool enough to rescue a stranger."

"You could let me go and claim that I escaped," she offered.

"Or you could be my hostage and I'll turn you over to the police when I know for certain that you are a terrorist."

"And how will you know that?"

"I don't know yet." Maddox pulled the hood of his parka up over his head and slid his hands into the gloves. "For now, you'll stick with me."

She opened her mouth to disagree, but he cut her off with a raised hand.

"No argument." He grabbed her elbow in his hand and ushered her off the porch and across the snow-covered yard toward the barn.

Once inside, he bypassed the horses and headed for the two snowmobiles parked in an empty stall. He laid the bag on the back of one snowmobile, securing it with flexible cords.

Katya shivered. The cool air had nothing to do with the chill spiraling down her spine. The last time she'd been on a snowmobile, she'd almost lost her life. That

and the amount of animosity radiating from Maddox
made her want to run away as far as she could get. From
warm, caring rescuer to tall, cold stranger, filled with
nothing but anger and accusations. He was breaking her
heart.

How? How could a man—practically a stranger—
have such a hold on her emotions? Was it some psycho-
logical attraction she felt for him because he had rescued
her? It had to be.

It could not be because he was so tall, strong and
earthy, the exact opposite of the men she was used to.
Or that he accepted the risk of rescuing her, placing his
own life in danger. And he had rescued her again when
she had been kidnapped.

"Rescuing me is becoming a habit for you, isn't it?"
she stated, more to herself than to him.

Maddox shot a glance her way and, without responding, walked to the opposite end of the barn and flung
open the back door. A gust of wind whipped through the
barn, carrying with it a spray of snow. Then he climbed
onto one of the machines and cranked the engine, backed
it out of the stall and drove it through the door. "Hop
on."

She crossed the interior of the barn, pulling the collar
of her jacket up around her neck. "Shouldn't I ride on
another?"

"No. I don't trust you on your own." He dismounted
and closed the barn door behind her, before resuming
his seat on the machine.

"I see." Katya stood, anxiety and something else
burning low in her gut. "What if I don't want to ride
with you?"

"Tough."

She could not imagine riding behind Maddox, her arms wrapped around him. "And if I refuse?"

"If you refuse to come with me, I'm sure Sheriff Yost would love to add you to the scalps on his belt." His brows raised. "What's it going to be?"

Knowing there was only one answer to his question did not make it any easier for her to give in. She was not known for her easy acceptance of any awkward situation. Her father had called her stubborn. But the choice was clear. She couldn't go with Yost or she would be thrown in jail, no one the wiser for who had actually planted the weapons in her apartment.

If she was to be Maddox's hostage, she had to convince him to help her find the real terrorist—the one who wanted her dead or at least so buried in the penal system that she couldn't get out to go home to Trejikistan. If she could not convince Maddox to help her, she had to find a way to escape from him and get back to Minneapolis to get answers to this mess on her own.

Katya slung her leg over the backseat of the snowmobile, keeping as far away as she could from actually touching Maddox. She could not risk letting her guard down with him. He did not trust her and because of that, she could not trust him. With what seemed like an entire country on the lookout for her as a suspected terrorist, she did not see how she would find the real culprit without help. But she would manage, or die trying.

Maddox revved the engine and shot out of the barnyard, careful to keep the barn between him and the ranch house for as long as possible, thus lessening the chance of being seen or heard until they were too far away for the sheriff to give chase in his pickup.

At first Katya refused to hold on to him, but as they

bumped across the drifts of snow, she was nearly unseated several times and finally grabbed him around the waist, holding on as tightly as she could.

A certain sense of justice filled Maddox, along with a rising need to feel her body against his. She'd been a mystery to him from the first time he'd laid eyes on that damn red scarf blowing in the wind. And nothing she'd said or done had cleared up the mystery surrounding her since. He'd be damned if he let her go until he figured her out. If that meant holding her hostage until she came clean, so be it.

They sped across the expanse of snowy terrain, putting as much distance as possible between them and the sheriff.

"Where are we going?" Kat yelled over the roar of the snowmobile engine.

He didn't answer, letting her guess, as she'd had him guessing since they'd met. That little bit of payback did nothing to settle the thrumming in his veins, the adrenaline kick he couldn't set aside in anticipation of their destination.

An hour later, fingers cold and Kat clinging to him to keep warm, Maddox pulled up to a small log cabin out in the middle of the frozen tundra. He parked the snowmobile behind the cabin in a lean-to built for that very purpose.

"What is this place?" Katya stood, stretching stiffly, tucking her hands beneath her armpits for warmth.

"The family hunting cabin. We come out here during the fall and stay for a week."

"Why here?" She looked back the way they came.

"Hard to find and harder to get to if you don't know where you're going."

The logs were old and weathered a dull gray, the door made of planks held in place by a combination lock. Maddox removed a glove and tumbled the combination, twisting it left then right until it fell open. He removed the lock and opened the door.

The inside was as gray as the outside, only darker. A small table, one rickety chair, and a rough-hewn bed made of carved wood posts with rope strung across was the extent of the furniture. A fireplace, lined with river rock, filled one end of the cabin. Next to it was a footlocker, which could be used as a second chair.

Maddox tossed the bundle he'd brought onto the bed. "There's canned food in the footlocker, see what you can find while I bring in the firewood."

When she didn't move, he stared across the floor. "You do know how to cook, don't you?"

"Yes, yes. Of course I do." Katya hurried toward the box on the floor and lifted the lid.

Once outside, Maddox collected logs. Being alone in the cabin with Katya brought back way too many memories of their night in the cave, memories best left in cold storage. The more time he spent alone with her, the less he was able to rein in his libido. The woman was hot, in or out of all the winter clothing. And one bed between them spelled trouble. Thank goodness they wouldn't be there the entire night.

Grateful that his family kept the cabin stocked, Maddox carried a full load of wood inside and laid it by the fireplace.

Still wearing her coat, and blowing steam as she breathed in and out, Katya had opened a can of beans with the manual can opener they kept in the footlocker.

Beside it was the pot they would hang over the fireplace to heat their food.

"See, I'm not completely useless. But I do need to relieve myself. Are there any facilities I can make use of?"

Maddox glanced over at her, attributing her inability to make eye contact to her embarrassment over asking about a bathroom. "There is an outhouse behind the cabin."

Her brows furrowed.

"An outhouse is an outdoor bathroom. It's either that or expose yourself to nature and the biting wind."

"I'll risk the outhouse." Her forehead smoothed. "Thank you for everything, Maddox." With that, she turned and left the cabin.

Something about the way her last statement came across didn't sit right with Maddox. He tossed the kindling he held into the fireplace and straightened. As he did, a distinct rasp of metal on metal was accompanied by a sharp click.

In the back of his mind, Maddox knew it wouldn't be there, yet he looked at the table where he'd laid the combination lock when he'd come into the cabin the first time. The table was empty.

"Katya!" Maddox raced for the door and shoved the bolt to the side. When he pushed on the door, it remained closed. "Dammit, woman, unlock the door!"

"I will not let you be held responsible for my predicament. This way they will know that I tricked you."

Maddox dragged in a deep breath and let it out, counting to ten at the same time. In as calm a voice as he could manage with anger and panic warring within him, he said, "Katya, don't do this. It's almost dark. You'll get lost on the prairie."

"It is a chance I have to take to keep you and your family out of trouble with the law." She paused. "I won't forget you, Maddox. Thank you for helping me when I needed it most. Thank you for…everything."

His heart pounding in his ears, Maddox hit the door, hard. The metal latch held.

"Katya!"

Chapter Ten

The cabin door shook with the force of Maddox slamming against it.

Katya jumped away, afraid the metal latch wouldn't hold under the force of his weight and anger.

Her heart thundering, she raced around the cabin to the lean-to in the rear. She hoped Maddox had left the keys in the ignition of the snowmobile. Without them her attempt to escape would be hopeless. An hour away from the ranch house, she could not possibly make it back to a highway to hitch a ride before nightfall. As it was, darkness descended on North Dakota early in the winter, making it difficult to see in the shadows of the overhang. To add to her dilemma, clouds covered the sky, negating any possibility of starlight to navigate by.

"Katya!" Maddox's angry cries thundered through the solid log walls.

Katya straddled the snowmobile and ran her fingers across the controls, searching in the dark for a key or starter switch.

As her hands closed around the key, a great crash sounded behind her.

With her breath lodged in her throat, Katya turned

the key and the engine revved to life. She jammed the gearshift into Reverse and backed out of the shed.

Once clear, she shifted into Drive. As she twisted the handle, giving the engine a quick burst of fuel, something heavy landed on the back of the machine, arms closing around her waist.

She screamed, her hand letting go of the throttle.

Maddox's arms circled her waist and yanked her off the seat and into a pile of snow.

She landed with a jolt on top of Maddox. He held tight, taking the brunt of the landing.

The snowmobile slid to a stop, the engine humming, but the machine motionless with no gas to power the tracks.

"Let go!" she yelled. "This is the only way to keep you safe."

"No way. Not until I know everything."

"How can you know everything when I don't even know it?" She struggled, kicking and flailing like a turtle on its back, unable to gain purchase.

"Will you be still?" Maddox grunted.

"No! I need to get out of here. I have to find out who is doing this to me."

"Be still, dammit!" He shoved her off him, letting go for just a moment.

Taking her only chance left, Katya leaped to her feet and ran for the snowmobile.

Before she had gone two steps, Maddox tackled her, taking her down in one inglorious heap, facefirst in the snow. The wind knocked out of her, she could not move or fight him off. He flipped her over and straddled her hips, pinning her hands over her head in the snow.

"No. More. Running," he said through gritted teeth, glaring down at her.

Katya stared up into his eyes. Completely immobile, captured by her rescuer and powerless to escape. He outweighed her and could easily fend off any attempt she made at fighting him. Defeated, she gave in, hopelessly hostage to the way he made her feel. "I never meant for this to happen."

The lines across his forehead eased, his gaze shifting from her eyes to her lips. "Neither did I." Then he was kissing her, his lips slanting across hers, his tongue pushing past her teeth to twist and taste, thrusting past her defenses.

Determined to remain immune to him, Katya felt her resolve dissolve under his savage onslaught. She couldn't feel the cold snow on her backside for the heat burning within. She couldn't fight him…she didn't want to. This was where she'd wanted to be since their first night together in the cave.

When he lifted his face, she gathered air into her lungs and made one last attempt at reason. "You should not get involved with me."

"I know." He smoothed a tendril of hair out of her face. "And yet I can't help myself." His gaze broke contact with hers and he stared around at the snow as though just becoming aware of his surroundings. "Come on, it's getting cold." He climbed to his feet and extended a hand to her.

She laid her gloved hand in his and he pulled her up against his chest.

With his arm like an iron band around her waist, he stared down into her eyes, his gaze fiercely determined. "Promise me that you won't try to run again?"

"Being with me puts you in danger."

"*Kitala igmu taka,* little lion." His jaw tightened. "Promise."

After the past couple days on the run, alone and without anyone to call for help, Katya couldn't resist Maddox's strength. "I cannot continue to rely on you to protect me. You have your own life, and getting involved with me could ruin it."

"Let me worry about that." His gaze never wavered from hers.

Katya sighed, leaning her forehead into his chest. "I promise."

For a brief moment, his arm tightened, then he moving her away from him. "I'll take care of the snowmobile."

Without his arms around her, the cold crept beneath her jacket, making her shiver. As Maddox climbed aboard the still-humming machine, Katya looked on with a mix of regret and relief. Finding her way across the frozen North Dakota Badlands in the dark had been a foolish idea, one born of desperation and panic.

Maddox spun the snowmobile around and parked it beneath the lean-to, purposely pulling the keys from the ignition and dangling them for her to see before he tucked them into his pocket. He led her to the front of the cabin and stepped inside.

Katya entered the cabin, noting the splintered latch where the lock had been until Maddox busted through. "I am sorry about the lock."

"It can be fixed." He knelt by the fireplace, arranging the kindling and then striking a long wooden match across the stones. Before long a small fire burned, casting an intimate glow in the tiny cabin.

She turned away, forcing herself to think, to reason away the yearning she could not seem to deny. Ever since her mother died, she had taken on the role of hostess for thousands of diplomatic dinners and meetings, all the while longing for the freedom to be herself, to be alone with only one man. A man of her choosing.

A smile curved her lips. Funny how this man had not been of her choosing. The situation had chosen him for her. Yet she could think of no other she would rather be stranded with on a windswept prairie.

Heat spread through the cabin and pulsed throughout her body, carried by a rapidly increasing heartbeat.

How could she keep her distance from Maddox Thunder Horse, the tall, dark Native American hero who'd saved her from death not once, but twice? Despite her determination to keep her distance, Katya glanced toward him.

His back to her, he was staring down into the fire. His presence filled the room, broad shoulders, blocking the light cast by the fire, silhouetted with the blaze bright between his spread legs.

He unzipped his jacket and tugged it from his shoulders.

Katya caught her breath as his muscles flexed beneath the stretchy cotton of the long-sleeved shirt he wore. Her fingers tingled at the memory of his smooth, dark chest beneath her hands, the way his skin tasted on her lips. That moist place between her thighs throbbed, achingly aware of his every movement.

When he turned toward her, she could not drag her gaze from his, could not hide what could only be longing shining from her eyes.

Maddox stared across the cabin at Katya. The faint

glow of the fire reflected in her ice-blue eyes and gave her black hair a soft shine, highlighting the waves. Even bundled in her winter coat, the woman held herself like a queen—regal, elegant and yet fragile in the sparse surroundings of the hunting cabin.

Every fiber of Maddox's being cried out to protect this small woman—from the ravages of the weather to the violence of the man determined to abduct her.

When she'd locked him in the cabin, panic catapulted his anger, pushing adrenaline through his veins like pressurized steam. Every possible scenario that could happen to her erupted in his mind, none with a good outcome. First and foremost was Katya lost in the Badlands, only to be found too late to help, her frozen face staring up at him. Her image merged with his memory of Susan.

"What do we do now?" she asked, her voice a hushed whisper in the confines of the tiny cabin.

Maddox could think of a lot of things they could do to pass the time. But he didn't want to scare her or take advantage of her after her tumble in the back of the wrecked car. "You could start by telling me everything you've been hiding from me."

"You already know I've been framed."

"Why?"

"I don't know." Katya turned away.

Maddox closed the distance between them. "I think you do." His arms circled her waist and he drew her back against his front. "Tell me."

At first she remained stiff in his arms. After a long moment, she leaned into him. "My father was…" she hesitated, then continued "…an important political figure in Trejikistan, my homeland, formerly part of

Russia. I received word two weeks ago that he was involved in an accident. There was no accident. He was murdered, and I think the people who murdered him are after me."

"But why set you up as a terrorist?"

"So that if they do not manage to kill me, I could never return to Trejikistan and carry on my father's legacy."

"I thought you were just a student."

"I am...I was, until my father's death. I just wanted to have a normal life, to blend in and be a student, not a political figure with an entourage of paparazzi following me around the rest of my life. I wanted to be me." Her voice dropped to a whisper on the last word.

Maddox turned her in his arms.

She gave little resistance, laying her cheek against his shirt, her fingers curling into the fabric. "Just me."

He tilted her chin and looked down into her eyes, amazed at how brave she'd been under the circumstances. No matter how badly he wanted to push her away and believe the worst, he couldn't. He might be the biggest fool ever, but he wanted to believe her story.

"I'm tired of crying," she said, looking up into his face. "And I'm tired of running." Her chin hardened, her lips pressing into a thin line. "If you want to help me—and I am not asking you to—I need to get back to Minneapolis and find out who planted those weapons in my apartment."

"Are you sure you want to go back where you're probably on everyone's watch list?"

"I have to." Her gaze raked his face. "Do you not see? If I do not, the police will crucify me. I am a foreigner, the media will try to convict me without bothering to get their facts straight. I will never be able to go home again." Her hands clenched in the fabric of his shirt. "My father's death will remain an *accident* while a killer runs loose out there. Whoever did this will win."

For a long moment, Maddox stared down into those bottomless blue eyes. "If I agree to help you, will you agree to do it my way?"

Her brows dipped slightly. "You know you will be labeled an accessory to whatever crime they pin on me. Are you willing to take that risk?"

He nodded. "You didn't answer my question."

The frown furrowing her brow lifted. "I will do it your way."

"Good." Maddox still held her in his arms. "That wasn't so hard, was it?"

Katya sighed. "I still do not like that you are involved."

"I made that decision, not you." He brushed a lock of raven-black hair from her forehead. "Get over it."

"I am finding it very difficult to get over it as far as you are concerned." Her eyelids drooped, the long, lush lashes shadowing her pale irises. When her tongue swept across her full dusky-rose lips, Maddox couldn't hold back.

He had to taste her, touch her lips with his own. His fingers rose to cup the back of her head, lacing through the long, luxurious layers of hair. When his mouth descended onto hers, he took her slowly in a deliberate kiss, one meant to explore, discover and learn everything there was to know about this woman in his arms. He knew so little about her, and he longed to know more. From her favorite color to the name of her first pet, to the places on her body that made her crazy with desire.

Maddox's groin tightened and he pulled away. He wanted her so badly, he was afraid it would cloud his judgment.

Katya's arms circled his neck and drew him back down to her mouth. "Is this part of doing it your way?" She pressed her lips to his. "Because if it is, I will agree to more of this—no argument."

A chuckle rose up his throat and he kissed her hard, before setting her away from him. "You aren't obligated to kiss me."

Her brows winged upward. "Do you think I kissed you out of obligation?" She unzipped her jacket and let it fall to the floor. "My reactions to you have never been those of one who feels obligated." She closed the short distance between them. "More a sense of the inevitable." She stared up at him. "Do you kiss me out of obligation?"

Maddox snorted. "No." His gaze captured her stormy one, his pulse racing, his hands aching to take her back into his arms, but he refused to make the first move this time. If she wanted what he wanted, she'd have to tell him. Taking her, making love to her in this tiny cabin might be the biggest mistake of his life. This woman could be a master spy, a consummate liar, a terrorist for all he really knew about her. But if she took him into her arms and kissed him, she would have conquered him completely, undermined his ability to resist.

Katya's gaze retained its hold on his. "My father never let me be with men he deemed unsuitable. He kept a very tight rein on my activities, not that I would disappoint him in any way."

"And your father would deem me unsuitable."

She curled her fingers around the hem of her sweater

and pulled it up and over her head, tossing it onto the table. "Probably. You do not provide any political value to the equation. You are not from Trejikistan or one of its neighboring countries." She unzipped the snowpants she'd borrowed from his mother and slid them down her legs. "You do not own a fleet of ships or oil wells." Her fingers tugged the button loose on the jeans she wore beneath, flicking it open.

His breath caught and lodged in his throat as her jeans followed the snowpants to the floor.

"You do not have any major political connections. You would be unworthy of my affiliation." Katya strode across the floor, wearing nothing but a black lace bra, panties and the pendant she fingered now.

Maddox's heart fluttered, the ache intensifying in his groin. "You know how to build a man up, don't you?" She didn't have to say a word to make him hot.

"I did not say that I agreed with my father." She stopped in front of him and ran her fingers down his chest to the button of his snowpants. "I loved my father. But he was, after all, a father looking out for the best interests of his only daughter."

"And you found his scrutiny too confining?"

"Yes." She unzipped the pants and pushed them down his legs.

Maddox stepped out of them and kicked them to the side. "And now that your father can't call the shots?"

Her hands paused on the rivet to his jeans. She closed her eyes and sucked in a ragged breath. "I miss him."

Maddox's hand closed over hers. "Don't do this just because you can."

Katya opened her eyes and stared up at Maddox. "I've

been a student in your country for six months. I could have made love to a dozen men by now."

"And have you?"

"No."

"Why me?"

She didn't step away, didn't remove her hand from his jeans. Instead, she stared up into his face. "I don't know. For some reason, you make me feel as though I am living life for the very first time."

That cold lump in his chest he'd given up on when Susan died swelled, filling and expanding to accommodate the blood flowing swiftly through his veins. The rush of emotion was quickly chased by panic. "And you make me feel…again. And frankly that scares the hell out of me."

She raised her hands to his cheeks. "I'm sorry about your fiancée. That must have hurt a lot."

He nodded, unable to voice the amount of pain he'd experienced at the time. His fingers tightened in her hair. "I can't do that again. I won't." His jaw clenched, his teeth grinding away at his memories.

"You don't have to." Her smile softened, her blue eyes swimming in a film of unshed tears. "I cannot stay in your country, anyway. Once I clear up this mess, I have to return to my home."

She'd left him an out. The opportunity to make love with no regrets, no ties, no claim on this woman, or her on him. He didn't have to invest his emotions as he had with Susan.

But what if he wanted to? "Do you have to go back?"

She nodded, her fingers stroking his stubbled chin. "Yes."

He sucked in a deep breath to steady his heartbeat, hoping he could turn it back into stone, although he feared it was too late. "Well, then, we'd better get some sleep." Maddox pulled her arms down from his face and stepped away from her tempting body, clad only in her underwear. It cost him.

Dearly.

"Sleep?" She stared at him, her breasts rising and falling behind the black lace, her arms wrapping around her middle, covering the rising goose bumps.

"Sleep." He nodded to where the sleeping bag lay spread across the ropes strung between the hand-carved bedposts. "You can have the bed."

She glanced at the bag, a shiver wracking her body.

Maddox wanted to take her back in his arms and warm all parts of her body, but he dared not. He couldn't afford to put his arms around her. If he did, he was afraid he'd never let her go. And she'd made it plenty clear to him that she was not sticking around.

One by one, she gathered her clothes.

His pulse thundering in his veins, his body stiff and ready for what he knew he couldn't have, Maddox couldn't watch. He turned his back to her and stirred the logs in the fire, the flames flaring up, sending a shower of sparks across the floor.

She'd done that to him. Stirred the embers in his heart and made him want the flame again. How had he come to this? How had he let himself feel for a woman again? Especially one who came with so much baggage and promised she'd be leaving.

Damn her!

Chapter Eleven

Katya dressed in her jeans and sweater before crawling between the folds of the sleeping bag. She lay facing Maddox, silhouetted in the glow from the fire.

How she wanted to go to him and put her arms around him, bring him back to the bed to make love to her as they had in the cave. But that was before he knew she was an accused terrorist. Before he knew she'd be leaving soon. Before she knew she was falling in love with this tall, dark Native American, whose heart and family were tied to the North Dakota Badlands. Even if she wanted him to follow her back to Trejikistan, she couldn't let him.

She didn't know what awaited her there. With her country torn apart by warring factions, she would be in constant danger, forever looking over her shoulder. And how did she expect the people of her country to follow her when it had taken every ounce of political pull and diplomacy her father could muster to steer the people toward democracy? And what had it gotten him? He'd been murdered, probably by the very people determined to squelch the democratic movement and return a king to ultimate power.

Who would they choose as the leader? Who would

they put in power if Katya decided to stay in America? If she decided to abandon her country, her people?

She gathered the edges of the sleeping bag around her, the thick fabric unable to dispel the chill suffusing her body. Her life, her moral code, instilled by her father, dictated that she return to her country. Without a ruler to guide them, Trejikistan would become a military state. Whoever orchestrated her father's death would take power and ruin the people's chances of a democracy.

As her father's daughter and until her brother returned, she was next in line to rule Trejikistan. She had to assume her position and responsibility at least until the elections the following spring.

Maddox poked at the fire, his broad shoulders flexing and retracting with each movement.

The temptation to go to him grew stronger with each passing minute. If she hoped to get any sleep whatsoever, she couldn't continue to watch him. Forcing herself to be reasonable, she turned over in the bag, turning her back to Maddox and the alluring glow of the fire. She stared at the dark, bleak walls, so cold from the temperatures outside. Even if she didn't go to sleep, she could rest. She'd need to be ready to go whenever they made their next move.

With the pendant her father gave her clutched between her fingers, her eyelids drooped and she fell into a troubled sleep.

Trapped in a canyon, giant boulders blocking her path, forcing her into a maze she could not find her way out of, Katya ran. Her breathing came in ragged gasps, behind her a man with cold eyes followed, closing in on her location.

She ducked inside a cave, crouching low to the floor,

dragging in enough air to keep from passing out. When would this nightmare end? Surely it was only a dream. Soon she'd awaken in her own bedroom.

Katya closed her eyes and reopened them, hoping for the familiarity of her floral bedspread and the clock radio on her nightstand. Instead she awoke to her apartment filled with machine guns, blocks of plastic explosives and someone banging on the door.

"Police!" *someone yelled through the wood paneling.* "Open up!"

Katya closed her eyes again, wishing for escape, only to find herself back in the cave, the sound of footsteps running toward her. She had to get away. She couldn't let the murderer capture her—her family depended on her to clear their name. Her people depended on her to save them from a crushing military dictatorship.

Katya leaped to her feet and ran for the cave entrance, ready to stand up to the man chasing her or die trying.

As she emerged from the cave into the night air, hands grabbed her, pulling her against a rock-solid body. "No!" *she cried, beating her fists against her captor's chest.*

"Wake up, Katya!" *Her captor shook her.* "Wake up!"

Katya opened her eyes to the soft glow of fire in the fireplace and Maddox's worried gaze. Her struggles ceased, and she fell into his arms, her body shaking, exhausted.

"It's okay, you were only dreaming."

"But it felt so real." She buried her face in his neck, inhaling denim, leather and Maddox's fresh-soap smell. Her fingers clung to his shirt, clutching him close to her.

"You're safe for now," he crooned softly, his lips against her temple, his hand stroking her hair down her back. "You're safe."

"No, I am not." She moved closer, her body curling into his. "I will not be safe until the man chasing me is caught, or I am dead."

"I'm here. I won't let anything happen to you."

"You cannot promise that," she whispered into his neck, afraid to let go, lest she wake up to find he was never there.

"I can and do." Maddox's hand continued to stroke the back of her head, threading his fingers through her hair, trailing them down her back.

Slowly, her muscles relaxed and she let herself breathe again. "I cannot live this way."

"No one could. That's why we're going back to Minneapolis to figure this whole thing out."

"When?"

"Soon." He glanced at the watch on his wrist. "I arranged to meet my brother, Tuck, at the highway in a couple of hours when the coast is clear and the sheriff won't be awake to track us down."

She looked up into his face, loving the way the firelight enhanced the rich dark tones of his skin. "How did you arrange that? Does this cabin have telephone service?"

"No. I did it before we left." He stretched his legs out on the sleeping bag beside her, leaning against the cabin's log walls.

"You planned on helping me all along?" she asked.

"Yes."

His warmth spread throughout her body, chasing away the fear and dread from her dream. "Thank you."

"Don't thank me yet. We don't know what we have in store for us in Minneapolis."

"Still, you're putting your life on hold and in danger to help me." She leaned up and kissed his beard-roughened cheek. "Thank you."

Gratitude had nothing to do with her next kiss. She pressed her lips to his, loving the smooth fullness. The closer she moved, the closer she wanted to be to him.

He broke away, his hands still entangled in her hair, the rigid evidence of his arousal pressing into her thigh. "No, we shouldn't."

"No one knows that more than I do." She leaned forward and kissed him again.

"Someone needs to stop before we go too far."

"Would that be you?" she asked.

"Not this time. If you want this to end now, you'll have to say so. I've been wanting to do this since the cave." He laid her down beside him, nestled in the sleeping bag. Leaning over her, he kissed her so thoroughly he took her breath away.

Katya clung to him, her pulse quickening, her breath tight, short spasms, providing little relief to her oxygen-starved lungs. Her fingers shoved at the shirt he wore, pushing it up and over his head, her hands splaying over the hard planes of his chest, feverishly memorizing every contour. Later, when she made it back to her home country, she would have little more than her memories to keep her warm at night.

Her breath caught in her throat and a sudden welling of tears threatened to take over. Dammit, she was done with crying. She had shed enough tears in the past three days to last a lifetime. With so little time left with Maddox, she wanted nothing more than to seize the moment, experience everything she could before she went home—should she live long enough and bypass the legal system to get back.

Maddox tugged her shirt up over her head and flung it over the bedpost. Her jeans came next, then the scrap of silk underwear and lace bra. The chill air pebbled her skin and made her breasts form pointed peaks.

Maddox stared down at her, drinking in every detail. Her pale skin reflected the warm glow of the firelight, her hair held a sheen similar to moonlight on still water. Her legs parted, her knees falling to the sides, welcoming him.

He stripped off the rest of his clothing and crawled into the sleeping bag with her, covering her body with his, settling between her legs. His erection pressed against her opening, but he refused to dive in like an eager teenager.

Katya had insisted that she couldn't stay. Her words hurt more than Maddox cared to admit.

His revenge would come in the form of sensual torture. He lowered his lips to hers, poised a hair's breadth from the temptation of her kiss. When she leaned up to capture his lips, he pulled away.

Instead, he pressed a kiss to her nose, her forehead, her cheeks and trailed a line of tender caresses along her jawbone, nipping and tonguing the pulse at the base of her throat.

His hands smoothed along the regal line of her neck and downward, skimming across her collarbone, edging ever closer to her breasts.

Her back arched, bringing her breast in contact with his fingers.

He tweaked the rosy-brown nipples to a velvety peak, his fingers massaging until Katya moaned.

"Maddox, please." Her body writhed with each touch, her feet churning the sleeping bag into a tousled heap. Her fingernails scraped his buttocks, digging in, tugging him closer, urging him to fill her.

He resisted, letting his lips follow his fingers to her breasts, taking them into his mouth one at a time, tasting the luscious sweetness.

Katya's legs wrapped around his waist, her heels digging into his back. "Please, Maddox," she begged.

"Patience. I want to bring you with me."

"I am with you, oh, please. What you are doing is making me completely insane." Her words came out in breathy gasps. Her feet falling to the sleeping bag, her heels digging in, lifting her hips upward.

When he didn't think he could hold out any longer, Maddox slipped lower on the shifting rope bed, his knees digging into the sleeping bag, finding the gaps between the ropes. He levered himself lower, his tongue skittering across Katya's flat belly and lower to the apex of her thighs.

"Please come inside me, please," she begged, her fingers clutching at his hair in spasms.

He wasn't finished. His tongue delved between her folds, lapping at the swollen nub until her bottom rose off the bed and her fingernails pressed into his scalp.

Her body tensed, then a soft gasp whooshed from her lips. She clung to him, breathing hard.

Only then did he shift up her body and slide into her heated slickness. He thrust deep, riding the wave of his desire.

At last he catapulted over the edge, his body throbbing

to a rhythm as ageless as time. Spent, he collapsed over her, drawing her into his arms without severing the intimate connection.

Together they fell into a deep dreamless sleep, arms and legs intertwined, the sleeping bag pulled up around their shoulders as the fire died.

A loud roar and insistent beeping woke Maddox. He jerked away, stabbing at his watch to silence his alarm. It took several seconds for him to realize the sound was coming from outside the cabin. The roaring wasn't the wind but the revving of a snowmobile engine.

Maddox leaped out of the bed and dragged his jeans up over his hips.

"What's happening?" Katya sat up, clutching the bag to her breasts.

"I don't know."

"Maddox!" Tuck's voice called to him through the thickness of the wooden door.

Maddox grabbed his sweater and flung the door open, letting in a blast of arctic air. "Tuck, what are you doing here? Is it time already?" He glanced down at his watch, the icy wind against his exposed skin making him shake so badly he could barely see the digital numbers.

"Get your clothes on, someone alerted our favorite sheriff that Katya is a wanted woman. He's on his way out to check the hunting cabin."

"How did he know to come here?"

"Heck if I know. I heard it on the police scanner and hightailed it out here as fast as I could." Tuck nodded at Maddox's naked chest and glanced toward the dark interior of the cabin. "Better get her out of here before the sheriff arrives."

"What about the truck?" Maddox asked, tugging his sweater over his head.

"Dante's driving it to our designated location on the highway. He'll take the snowmobile back to the ranch. He didn't dare take the chopper out. As it is, he'll have enough explaining to do with the Border Patrol."

"I am ready when you are." Katya stepped up beside Maddox, zipping her jacket up to her neck.

Maddox could have kissed her already kiss-swollen lips. "Give me a second, and I'll meet you in back by the lean-to." He shut the door, blocking the wind from blowing through the already freezing cabin while he finished dressing in his cold-weather gear.

When he had his boots on and his hood pulled down over his head, he pulled Katya into his arms and kissed her. A quick, brief kiss, but it would have to do until he could kiss her again. And he planned on kissing her a hell of a lot more. So much so that she would change her mind about going back to Trejikistan. With her father dead, what could possibly make her want to return to a country that didn't want her back to begin with?

When Katya walked outside, the full force of the wind hit her, making her step back before she could get her balance. Each time she went out into the cold, it got harder. She'd give anything to sit in a sauna and ease the chill out of her bones. But now was not that time.

Maddox jogged ahead of her and backed the snowmobile out of the lean-to, dusting the snow off the seat.

Katya climbed on the back and looped her arms around his waist.

Without another word to his brother, Maddox raced off into the night, headed toward the highway where his other brother waited. Tuck's snowmobile kept pace at his right, neither rider using headlights.

Katya glanced behind her at the cabin, a dark shape barely illuminated by the sketchy starlight was intermittently revealed by the skittering of clouds across the heavens.

A light blinked on the horizon past the cabin, a tiny light, barely the size of a distant star—only this wasn't a star.

Katya's heart raced, her hands tightening around Maddox's waist. "We're being followed!" Katya yelled and pointed back at the light.

Weighed down by two people, the snowmobile could not outrun the one following. The best they could hope for was to stay ahead of him and arrive at the truck before he did.

Tuck's snowmobile pulled close and he shouted over the roar of the engine, "We should split up. Maybe he'll follow me."

Maddox nodded. "Don't go and get yourself shot. Mom would never forgive me."

"Don't worry. I'll take a punch for you, but forget the bullets."

Despite his words to the contrary, Katya would bet her life that Tuck would take a bullet for Maddox. The Thunder Horse brothers were a force to be reckoned with and they obviously loved each other, even if they did not say it outright.

Tuck split off and dropped back to intercept the other snowmobile.

Maddox opened his machine up full throttle and raced off across the snow-covered landscape.

The last time Katya had been on a speeding

snowmobile, racing away from the bad guy on her tail, she had gone over the edge into a canyon. Between peering around Maddox at what lay ahead and tracking the light of the snowmobile behind them, she could not be still on the backseat.

She wished they did not have to go quite so fast, but slowing down was not an option.

If the man following them was the sheriff, he would throw her in jail, and wait for Homeland Security to come get her and sort things out. And when they did, her quest to clear her name might as well be over. Who would think to look further than a foreigner?

If the person behind them was the man who had tried to kidnap her, she might not see the morning dawn.

Squelching her fear of speed, Katya buried her face in Maddox's back and held on. The bumps and dips were amplified by the speed, slamming them into the earth or making them go airborne off the snowmobile's seat.

Several times Katya nearly lost her hold on Maddox, her body flying into the air, only to crash down when the skids hit the hard-packed snow.

Even while trying to hold on to Maddox, Katya worried about Tuck. Whatever he was doing back there, the light had not wavered once. In fact, it was getting bigger. The vehicle was closing in on them.

Katya glanced ahead. Where was the highway and Dante with the waiting vehicle? Would they make it in time?

Another look behind and the light was closer still. Then Katya saw a shadowy form cross in front of the other snowmobile. Over the roar of the engine, a loud crack ripped through the air.

Starlight glinted off Tuck's snowmobile as he

swerved and raced back across the path of the other snowmobile.

Her breath lodged firmly in her throat, Katya could only watch with a dreadful sense of doom as another crack blasted through the air. Tuck's snowmobile veered to the right and slowed to a stop.

Had their pursuer shot him? Was Tuck bleeding to death in the frigid cold? "We have to go back. Tuck's hurt."

"We can't," Maddox insisted. "The truck's ahead. Once we reach it, I'll send Dante back for Tuck."

"It could be too late. He could bleed to death!" Katya pulled at Maddox's sleeve. "You have to go back. You can't leave him there to die!"

Chapter Twelve

Maddox wanted to turn around and go back for his brother, but he'd promised Katya that he'd keep her safe. He couldn't do that by driving back into bullet range of their pursuer.

Ahead the sporadic starlight reflected off something metallic. That something had better be the truck his brother, Dante, was bringing. When they got to the truck, Dante would go back and check on Tuck.

That is, if they made it there before their pursuer planted a bullet in Katya's back. The only saving grace was that the terrain was bumpy, and steady aim would be impossible. But that didn't rule out a lucky shot—or an unlucky one if it hit one of them.

A quick glance over his shoulder kicked up his pulse a notch.

The snowmobile behind them was catching up fast.

A loud bang sounded over the noise of his engine.

Katya's arms tightened around his waist, her face digging into his back.

Maddox would have zigzagged to make it harder for the shooter to use them as target practice, but anything other than a straight line would slow them enough for him to catch up. With the throttle wide open, Maddox pushed the snowmobile to its limits.

A small beam of light flashed out over the snow. Using a handheld flashlight, Dante guided them to the truck.

Like a sprinter racing past the finish line, Maddox didn't slow down until he passed the truck and put the body of the vehicle between him and the shooter.

Dante stood behind the truckbed, a rifle aimed at the oncoming snowmobile. He fired off a shot.

The pursuer swerved, killed the headlight and pulled a tight circle, regrouping now that the odds were stacked against him.

Maddox pulled the snowmobile up to the pickup and leaped off. "Tuck's down back there. Promise me you'll take care of him."

His brother's eyes narrowed, his grip tightening on the rifle. Their pursuer kept his distance, just out of range of Dante's rifle. Which meant he was also out of range to fire a pistol at Maddox and Katya. "I've got this covered. You get her out of here."

"That's the plan." Maddox opened the passenger door and, keeping his body below the outline of the truck, climbed in and cranked the engine to life.

Katya hesitated. "We cannot leave Tuck out there. He could be hurt."

"I'll take care of him," Dante said, his focus remaining on the snowmobile in the distance. "Go!" he barked.

Katya threw herself into the truck, keeping her head below the level of the windows.

Even before the passenger door closed, Maddox shoved

the gearshift into Drive and shot down the highway, slipping sideways on the snow-covered, icy road.

Katya looked over the top of the seat. "I think the snowmobile is following us. It is hard to tell, he still has his light off."

"Keep your head down. Until we get to the interstate highway, he has the advantage on these snowy back roads."

The truck skidded and bumped across the treacherous path.

Every few minutes, Katya sneaked a peek out the back windshield. "I can't see him."

Maddox didn't slow or lose focus. With the headlights of the truck reflecting off the snow, their night vision would be less than adequate past the manmade illumination. They had to make several turns to get to the highway. The snowmobile didn't. The shooter could cut across fields and head them off if he knew where Maddox was headed.

Katya sat quietly in the seat beside him, slumped low, her eyes wide, brows furrowed. "I hope your brothers are all right."

"They've been through worse." His words belied his own worry as he fought to keep the truck from sliding off the road and into the ditches.

As they neared the intersection of the county road and the main highway leading to the interstate, Maddox slowed to make the turn.

Serving as his lookout, Katya swiveled in her seat, panning the horizon. "On your left!" She ducked.

The snowmobile roared across the road in front of the truck. Instinctively, Maddox slammed on his brakes.

The truck skidded sideways, not slowing any sooner.

A loud pop ripped through the air and the driver's-side window shattered, spraying glass throughout the interior.

"Stay down!" he shouted. Something stung his arm, but Maddox didn't let go of his grip on the steering wheel. He straightened the truck and skidded through the T-intersection, aiming for the interstate, sure that if they could get there, the snowmobile wouldn't be able to keep pace.

On the straight road, Maddox pushed the truck as fast as he could, praying he wouldn't slide off the side. The frigid air blowing in from the shattered window took his breath away. He reached for the heater, twisting the knob to the highest setting to keep them from getting frostbite. Lights reflected off the low-hanging clouds that had moved in from the west—it had to be the small town of Dickinson.

With hope in sight, Maddox increased his speed. As they neared the town, the road had less and less snow until all that was left was the sand and salt used by the highway department.

"I think we lost him," Katya said, looking through the rear window.

Houses and businesses lined the road into the town, and towering lights lit the interstate.

Katya touched Maddox's arm. "If the sheriff knows about me, he will have put out a message to all the law enforcement agencies, especially those along the main routes."

"You're right. Having a busted window won't help, either." Maddox slowed the truck and pulled down a side street, taking a less conspicuous route to the interstate. "We have to ditch the truck."

"How will we get to Minneapolis? Do they have a bus station here?" Katya asked.

"No, they have something better—truckers." Maddox parked two streets away from a well-lit truck stop and behind a large Dumpster.

Maddox dropped down out of the truck and rounded the vehicle to Katya's side. He opened the door and held his hand out to her.

She reached for it, but drew back, her forehead wrinkled. "Maddox, you're bleeding!" Katya slipped out of the truck without his help, her gaze on his arm with the blood-soaked sleeve. "We have to get you to a hospital."

He hadn't realized that he'd been hit. The shattering glass and the wild ride hadn't given him time to think about anything other than getting them to safety. "We don't have time. Besides, it's just a flesh wound." He touched his hand to the wound and fought back a wince. "Let's find a ride." He hooked her arm with his good one and led her toward the truck stop.

As they neared, Katya dug her heels into the pavement. "You cannot go in there. With all the blood, someone will get suspicious. They might call the police."

Maddox frowned. "You're right. But we can't risk you going in. What if they have fliers with your picture on them? If there are any cops in there, you could be caught."

"We'll have to take that chance."

"I'll sneak in and wash up in the bathroom."

"You'll need help."

"Here," Maddox dug in his back pocket and removed his wallet. He handed her a couple of twenties. "Buy a hat to cover your hair and face as much as possible. Get some bandages and meet me at the bathroom door in five minutes."

Katya nodded, accepting the money, her bottom lip caught between her teeth. "Are you sure you are okay?"

"Yeah. As far as I can tell without looking, the bleeding's stopped. I'll be fine. Just stay away from cops." He leaned close and brushed her cheek with his lips. "See ya in five."

Katya tucked the money into her snowpants pocket and entered the building through a side door. The truck stop had a store on one side and a restaurant on the other.

Through the front window, Katya spotted two county sheriff's cars parked along the curb. Her heart pounded against her chest as she moved through the aisles, keeping her head lowered. She found a rack of knitted hats in soft pastel colors. She chose one in rose and gray, colors so very different from her own hair color. Then she found the row with the first aid items, grabbed a box of gauze and medical tape and hurried to the counter to pay, careful to avoid contact with anyone. From the corner of her eye, she located the bathrooms between the restaurant and the convenience store. Now all she had to do was pay and get to Maddox.

A man asking for cigarettes got to the clerk first. Katya stood behind him, her head down, her gaze fixed on the floor.

As she waited her turn, a pair of brown boots appeared beside her. In her peripheral vision she could tell that the man wore brown trousers as well. The same color worn by Sheriff Yost.

A quick glance upward confirmed her guess. A

sheriff's deputy stood beside her, talking to another man in uniform behind him.

At last the man with the cigarettes paid for his purchase and left.

Katya laid her items on the counter, praying that the lawmen wouldn't question her need for gauze and tape. The men were so deep in conversation, maybe they'd completely ignore her.

The one closest to her was saying something about an APB. "Sheriff Yost issued it a couple hours ago. We're supposed to be on the lookout for some Russian woman suspected of terrorism."

Katya's heart skipped a beat at the man's words. She struggled against the urge to run, before the officers realized the woman they were supposed to be watching out for was right in front of them.

The clerk lifted the knit cap. "Ma'am, the hats on the other rack are half off."

"That's okay," she said, keeping her voice low and as American sounding as she could. She had practiced the American accent, wanting to fit in at school. "I like this one."

"There's one just like it on the other rack. Well, almost. Want me to get it for you?" The clerk stepped away from the register.

"No," Katya said, desperate to pay and leave the deputies behind. "I want this one."

The young man shrugged. "Have it your way. But the others are cheaper." He rang up the purchases and took the twenty she handed to him.

Her heart thumping wildly in her chest, Katya tried to fake a calm she didn't feel.

"Not from around here, are you?" the deputy beside her said.

Katya jumped, but refused to make eye contact with the man talking to her, preferring to fix her gaze on the clerk. "Nope," she said as quietly as she could.

"Where ya from?" he asked.

The man behind him elbowed him. "Give it up, Swenson. She's not interested."

The deputy closest to her turned to his friend, a fierce frown pulling his brows down over his eyes. "Shut up, Roe. Let the lady decide." The deputy faced her again. "Ignore the jerk. Where are you from?"

Remembering a movie she'd seen with her neighbor, she forced a response she hoped sounded genuine. "Jersey," she said, laying on the thick Jersey accent from the movie. Thankfully, the clerk handed her change to her. Relieved beyond reason, Katya was about to make her escape.

The clerk smiled at her and delayed her further with, "Really? What part? I have relatives in New Jersey."

Caught in her own lie, Katya's mind went blank. She couldn't remember the name of a single city in New Jersey.

As she groped for a response, the clerk tipped his head to the side. "Newark, I think. My cousin lives in Newark. You from anywhere close?"

"Newark," she said, gathering her items.

"Need a bag for that?" the clerk asked.

"No, thank you."

"Hey, I'm off in thirty minutes." The young deputy said. "Care to have breakfast with me?"

"Sorry, my husband is waiting," she said and hurried toward the bathrooms and Maddox. Not until she ducked down the hallway and out of sight of the deputies did she draw a breath. Then it was only to have it yanked out of her when a hand grabbed her from behind and tugged her into the men's bathroom and one of the stalls.

Her face burning, Katya stood chest to chest with Maddox. "I cannot be in here. This is the men's bathroom. What if someone comes in?" Katya protested.

"We'll take that chance." He had his jacket and shirt off.

Katya's hands, full of the hat and bandages, pressed into his warm, smooth skin. Her breath caught now for another reason entirely.

"Good, you got bandages." Maddox smiled. "You took longer than five minutes."

"Couldn't be helped." Katya eyed the wound.

He had managed to clean the blood off his jacket and hung it on the back of the stall door. The edges of the cut were cleaned as well, but fresh blood oozed out.

"Here, hold these." She handed him the hat and box of tape. Ripping two sterile packages of gauze from the remaining box, she folded one into a tight pad and pressed it against the injury, then laid the other over the first. She held out her free hand. "Tape."

He handed her the box of tape. "Are you a nurse back in your country?"

"No, but I had a brother," she said. "He was constantly getting into scrapes."

"What do you mean *had?*" Maddox's forehead creased. "Did he die?"

"No," she answered too quickly. She refused to believe that her brother was dead. If he was, she had no other family but her cousin, Vladimir. In other words, she had no family. "No, he is not dead. We...I do not know where he is."

Maddox's lips turned up in a gentle smile. "You've misplaced your brother?"

"You could say that. I have not heard from him in months. But he is alive." She stretched a band of white tape over the top of the gauze. "He has to be."

"Now we're getting somewhere. You know that I have three brothers. I know that you have at least one. Any other family I should know about?"

"No. It was just me, my brother and my father." Her voice cracked on the last word and she fought to keep from shedding another tear. She ripped off another strip of tape and plastered it to the bottom of the gauze. "There, you were right. It was just a flesh wound. You probably need a tetanus shot to be safe."

"Yes, ma'am. As soon as you're safe." He smiled down at her. "Thanks." Then he kissed her nose.

How she could get all hot and bothered by a man kissing her nose, Katya did not know, but she could not stop the rush of blood to the lower regions of her belly. She pressed closer to him, her hands sliding over his dark-skinned chest. "I do not understand why I cannot keep my hands off you."

"You don't hear me complaining." He captured her fingers in his and drew them up to his lips where he kissed her fingertips. "Much as I like what you're doing to me, we have to get out of here."

"Right." Katya said, dragging her focus back to the more immediate need for transportation. "And there are a couple of sheriff's deputies out there."

The outer door to the bathroom swung open.

Katya stepped up on the edge of the toilet seat and

squatted down so that whoever came in wouldn't see two sets of legs in one stall.

The door next to them opened and closed.

Maddox pressed a finger to his lips, slipped his shirt and jacket on, then slid the lock open on his stall door. Before she could guess at his next move, he grabbed her around the legs and lifted her up.

She swallowed a scream and held on as he carried her through the stall door to the exit.

Once outside the door, he dropped her on her feet. He took the hat from her hands and stretched it down over her hair, tucking the long strands up underneath. "There. Now we have to find a ride."

Maddox led the way through the restaurant, head down, eyes averted to avoid being recognized.

The deputies were sitting in a booth in the far corner, laughing over coffee and breakfast. The one who had hit on Katya looked up, his eyes narrowing at Maddox.

Pretending she didn't see him, Katya moved on to another booth as far away from the deputies as possible.

A group of truckers sat between Katya and the deputies, their loud voices and laughter enough to drown out any conversation Maddox and Katya might attempt.

"Aren't you afraid the deputies will question us?"

"We won't find out where the trucks are going if we don't eavesdrop on the conversations."

Katya sat with her back to the lawmen. Maddox faced them and the truckers. He stared toward Katya while he surreptitiously studied the truckers.

"Haven't seen the wife in a week." An older gentleman with a weathered face and graying hair twisted his coffee cup in his hands.

"Lucky dog." The man with his back to Maddox, with

strawberry-blond hair and freckles running together on his arms and neck, waved at the waitress with his mug.

"Unlike you dirtbags, I actually like my wife." The older man sipped his coffee and grimaced. "She makes a better cup of coffee than this swill."

"You're probably the only man I know who still gives a crap about his ball and chain." The man in the booth beside the older gentleman had the gravelly voice and heavily lined face of a smoker.

The gray-haired trucker shrugged. "She puts up with me and she's still as pretty as the day I met her."

The waitress swung by with a steaming pot of coffee.

"Where is this wife of yours?" The younger, freckled man set his mug on the table for the waitress to fill. "Might need to pay her a visit while you're out of town."

The men all laughed.

"She's out of your league, Red."

"How do you know?"

The man in the booth beside the freckled man, nudged him in the side. "Any woman in her right mind would be out of your league."

Ignoring the younger men's antics, the gray-haired man looked over at the smoker. "Where ya headed?"

"Spokane."

"I'm going the other direction." The older man stirred sugar into his coffee. "I'll be in Chicago by nightfall. Only have to make a quick stop in Minneapolis."

Katya's gaze connected with Maddox's and he mouthed the word *Bingo.*

After topping off the truckers' coffee mugs, the

waitress stopped beside Katya. "You want a menu, or do you already know what you want?"

Maddox stood, keeping his torn sleeve out of sight of the deputies in the corner. "We've changed our minds. Come on, darlin'."

The waitress shrugged. "Don't blame you, the food here sucks."

Katya slid out of the booth and preceded Maddox out of the restaurant and into the convenience store.

Without saying a word, Maddox purchased shrink-wrapped breakfast biscuits and a couple bottles of orange juice, all the while keeping a watch on the gray-haired trucker in the restaurant. Whether or not he knew or liked it, the old guy was their ticket to Minneapolis.

As he paid the clerk, Maddox could see the trucker zipping his jacket and pulling on his gloves.

"Come on, we have a bus to catch." Maddox grabbed the plastic bag with their food and hurried toward the door leading out to where the truckers parked the big rigs.

"Bus?" Katya said, running to keep up with Maddox. "I thought you said we were not taking a bus."

"Just some American slang." He smiled and held out his hand. "Come on, let's get out of sight until our bus driver comes out."

Katya grinned and slipped her gloved fingers in his. Her eyes widened and her smile slipped when she looked past him. She tugged him hard and shoved him behind a large trailer.

"What? Was it something I said?" Maddox leaned over the top of Katya's head as they peered around the corner of the trailer at the county sheriff's car pulling up to the other two parked at the curb.

Sheriff Yost climbed out of the car and scanned the area.

Maddox and Katya ducked back behind the trailer. "We have to get out of here." He looked around the corner again. Their gray-haired potential bus driver stood talking to the sheriff, looking down at the paper in the sheriff's hands.

The older gentleman shook his head and took off across the parking lot toward the tractor-trailer rig where Maddox and Katya were hiding.

Maddox swore under his breath. The only man they'd found going their way had gotten the heads-up from the sheriff. What chance did they have now that he would let them in the truck?

Chapter Thirteen

"Sorry, folks, but this is as far as I can take you. From here, I'm on to Chicago." Chuck Goodman pulled the truck into a huge distribution center in the warehouse district of Minneapolis. He climbed down out of the truck and stretched.

Maddox descended to the pavement and reached up a hand to help Katya out of the tall vehicle. They met Chuck in front of the truck. "Thanks for giving us a ride this far."

"You guys did me the favor by keeping me company. I hope things work out for you two. You seem nice enough."

Maddox held out his hand to the older man and they shook.

Katya bypassed the hand and hugged the man's neck. If not for him, their trip might have ended at the truck stop. "Thank you for taking a chance on us."

"Probably wouldn't have if you weren't such a pretty little thing. Can't imagine you had anything to do with whatever stuff they found in your apartment. And even I've heard of the Thunder Horse Ranch. Makes me proud to know someone is looking out for the wild ponies of the Badlands." He shook Maddox's hand again.

"Your wife is a lucky woman, Chuck. I hope we meet again." Maddox waved and led Katya through the gates and out onto the sidewalk.

They left Chuck at the distribution center and hiked toward a convenience store they'd spied a couple blocks away.

"We can take a taxi or the city bus from there," Katya said.

"I want to make a call first."

"Tuck?" Katya shot a glance at him. "Why didn't you borrow the trucker's cell phone?"

"I didn't want any law enforcement officials tracing anything back to Chuck. He did us a favor giving us a lift."

"Right."

At the convenience store, Maddox purchased a throw-away cell phone for himself and one for Katya. "Just in case," he said.

Katya shoved the phone in her pocket and stared out the window of the store at the gray skies and traffic, praying the news was good from the Thunder Horse Ranch.

Maddox finished his call and joined her. "*Wanka-tanka* is looking out for Tuck. He's fine."

That little bit of news was such a relief it lifted some of the weight off Katya's shoulders. She couldn't have lived with herself if something bad happened to any one of the Thunder Horse clan.

"One more thing." Maddox paused, his lips pressed into a thin line. "I told Dante where we'd left the truck."

"And?"

"A man was murdered near the truck stop and his

car was stolen. The sheriff was all over it, blaming us for the murder and the theft."

Katya's stomach clenched. Another crime to add to her growing list. "If they catch me, I will be in jail for the rest of my life."

"You didn't kill anyone, Katya." His hands gripped her shoulders. "Look at me."

Her eyes opened and she stared up into the fathomless depths of his brown-black eyes.

"We'll get you through this."

"How?"

"I don't know, but you have to believe we'll make it through." He pulled her close and held her for a long moment. Then he put her away from him. "Just believe."

Katya stared out the store window, trying not to fall apart. She twisted the chain around her neck, remembering the day her father gave her the necklace—the day she left for school in the United States. He'd wanted her to have something to remember her family back home in Trejikistan. He'd had the thick, white-gold pendant engraved with the family crest. "So that I always know you are safe," he'd said. "And so that you always know where you belong."

And she belonged with her people now that her father wasn't there to protect them from the potential of an unwanted dictatorship. Katya could only guess at who had attempted the coup. Trejikistan was such a small blip on the American news radar that finding any information about the country's upheaval would be next to impossible. If only she could get to the internet again. When she'd been at the Medora library, she hadn't had time. At the very least she needed to check for her bodyguard's response. Perhaps her brother had made his way back home after hearing of their father's death. *If* he'd gotten word. *If* he was still alive. Katya prayed that her brother was alive.

In the meantime, she had to find out who was trying to frame and kill her.

A taxi pulled up to the curb in front of the store. Maddox circled her waist with his arm. "Ready?"

Ready to walk back into the apartment where all her troubles had begun just a few short days ago? No, Katya's chest tightened and the uncontrollable urge to run hit her, panic setting in. The last time she was there, someone had tried to grab her. Would the man who'd been following them find her here? After all the cross-country trekking, she'd have thought she'd shaken the pursuer.

Like a Pit Bull Terrier with his teeth dug in deep, her nemesis wasn't letting her go that easily.

Katya gave the taxi driver directions to the hair salon where she had her hair done, two blocks from her apartment complex. She pulled the knit hat down low over her forehead, the bulky yarn covering her dark brows. If the entire police force of Minneapolis was searching for her, she'd be discovered in no time.

"How will you find out who set you up?" Maddox broke into her thoughts, his voice low enough so the driver couldn't overhear.

"I'm not sure." She hadn't thought further ahead than arriving at her apartment complex alive. Now that they were this close, she didn't have a clue. "I suppose I could talk to the neighbors."

"Does the apartment have a security system?"

"Yes." Katya sat forward, remembering her father's

insistence on staying somewhere that had good security. He'd wanted her to be safe so far away from home. "The apartment complex has a high-end security system. Surely part of it consists of a camera and a digital history of that day."

"If we could get the historical videos, maybe we can find our real terrorist." Maddox grabbed her hands. "Do you know the security guards? Ever talk to them?"

"As a matter of fact, one of them is a friend of mine. Casey Reed. I set him up with my classmate." He was the man who'd helped her escape her attacker and hid her from the police.

"Perfect." Maddox sat back, staring out the window. "Maybe he'll get us in to see the videos."

Katya stared across the backseat at Maddox, her heart swelling in her chest. "Thank you, Maddox."

He turned toward her, his brow furrowing. "For what?"

"For helping me when you really should not." She leaned across the seat and kissed him full on the lips.

The kiss deepened, Maddox's hands circling behind her neck to draw her closer. His tongue thrust between her teeth.

Katya melted against him, wishing the kiss could last forever.

Not until the taxi driver cleared his throat did they break apart. The kiss was everything she could have hoped for and yet it broke her heart into a million pieces. Once she cleared her name, she would be on her way back to Trejikistan. Maddox would be half a world away.

Katya climbed out of the taxi and stood on the sidewalk, her mood as dreary as the Minneapolis winter.

She should not have kissed him, knowing they could never be more than acquaintances. The more physical contact she had with Maddox Thunder Horse, the harder it would be to say goodbye.

They took the side roads to the apartment complex arriving at the rear entrance. "We won't get in without my card key, and that's somewhere back in the canyon with the snowmobile," she said.

"Then we'll go around the front and wait for your friend."

"He works the midnight-to-noon shift. He should be leaving any moment. I have a better idea that won't be so conspicuous." Katya took his hand and, like lovers, leaned into him and guided him a block away from the apartment to a park within view of the front entrance, but shaded by the overhang of trees and bushes.

A metal park bench faced the street and gave them a good vantage point from which to watch for anyone entering or leaving the building.

Katya dropped onto the metal seat and tugged on Maddox's hand. "Sit."

Maddox complied, his glance panning the area. "Aren't you afraid your stalker will make an easy target of you?"

Katya's lips pressed into a line. "Hopefully, he is still back in North Dakota scratching his head." She patted her hat. "And with the disguise, hopefully, he will not know who I am."

"I want to know how he found you at the cabin."

"Maybe he followed the snowmobile tracks."

"I suppose he could have."

A man dressed in a security guard uniform exited the

apartment building, walking toward them, head down, hands tucked in his thick winter jacket.

Katya gripped Maddox's hand. "That's Casey."

Maddox stood, pulling Katya to her feet. "Let's get started."

"What if he is spooked by all the publicity about my being a terrorist?" Katya stared up into Maddox's eyes, pretending that she was his lover for anyone passing by. Her heart skipped a few beats when he leaned close.

With his lips close to her ear, he whispered, "We'll just have to convince him that you aren't."

Katya's stomach tumbled, all her nerves bouncing from his gentle breath on her neck.

Maddox straightened and stepped in front of the security guard, blocking his path. "Excuse me, sir, are you Casey Reed?"

Casey stopped abruptly and backed up a step. "Yeah, that's me."

Katya laid a hand on the man's arm. "Casey, I need your help."

The security guard stared down at her hand then into her face, his eyes widening, a grin spreading across his face. "Kat?"

She darted a glance around the street. "Yes, Casey, it's me, Kat."

Casey's gaze swept the area as well before returning to Katya. "Holy cow, Kat, where have you been? The entire Minneapolis police force and the FBI are all looking for you."

"I know."

Casey shook his head. "What happened? Where did all that stuff come from? Tell me all those weapons and explosives weren't really yours. I never believed it, but the media sounds so convincing."

"No, they weren't mine. I have no idea how the weapons got into my apartment. They were planted while I was out that morning."

"I knew it. When they told me all that stuff was yours, I didn't believe them. You're too nice to be a terrorist. That's why I helped you get away."

"I had to leave." Katya recalled the man who had jumped her on her way back to her apartment that fateful morning. "Someone tried to kill me, Casey. I have been running ever since."

Maddox broke into the conversation. "Look, we can't stand out in the open much longer. We need your help to clear her of the charges."

Casey nodded. "What can I do?"

Katya touched a hand to his arm. "You were on duty between eight and noon that morning. Did anyone deliver anything to the building?"

"The cops asked the same question. We had a furniture delivery scheduled for apartment 627 at nine." Casey ran a hand through his hair. "I watched from the monitor. Everything was on the up and up. They brought in a couch and a love seat. No boxes or anything else. That was all that was delivered that morning."

"Did you actually see them take the furniture to 627?"

"Yeah. They delivered at exactly nine o'clock. I remember because Mrs. Carmichael walks her Shitzu every morning at nine o'clock."

Maddox stared across at Katya. "We need to see the videos of the entrances to the building. If that was the only delivery, they had to have gotten the weapons in during that time."

Before Maddox finished speaking, Casey was shaking his head. "The Feds confiscated every video for the last six months you've lived here."

Katya's hopes sank. "All of them?"

"Were the videos on tape or on a hard drive?" Maddox asked.

"Everything is backed up from the hard drive to tape once a month," Casey said. "We'd just completed a backup when the Feds charged in. They took all the tapes."

Maddox stepped forward. "Do you wipe the videos from the hard drive when you back up to tape?"

"You know," Casey scratched his chin. "I believe we do it a week later, just in case one of the tapes is bad on the monthly backup."

Katya pulled in a deep breath and let it out, feeling lighter. "Can we look for that day, just in case the video is still on the hard drive?"

In the corner of her peripheral vision, Katya noted a Minneapolis city police car pulled up to a stop sign two blocks away. "We need to move this discussion inside." She hooked Casey's arm and moved toward the apartment building.

Casey resisted. "I can't take you in there now. My boss is filling in for me while I'm on lunch break. He doesn't expect me back for another fifteen minutes. Besides, he's very strict about who gets inside the control room."

Katya changed direction, leading the two men to a small bistro a block from the complex. "Then let's get you some lunch and we can plan our next move."

Fifteen minutes later, Casey walked out of the bistro, his steps swift, his gaze shooting from side to side.

Katya regretted having to involve Casey. If he were caught assisting her now, he too could be considered an accessory to a potential terrorist wanted by the police and the FBI. And the poor man was scared to death.

For that matter, Katya was scared. Walking into the apartment building set her up for capture. Casey had given her his master key card. While he searched for the video from that day, Katya and Maddox would perform some illegal activities of their own. It was too dangerous to enter her own apartment, but based on Casey's observation, the owners of 627 were out.

Maddox and Katya were going to check out the furniture they'd had delivered and inspect it for any anomalies.

Katya pulled her collar up over her chin and ducked her head as she strode past the cameras at the entrance and in the front lobby.

Casey's boss had left shortly after he returned from lunch, but they didn't need to leave clear evidence of their visit on the videos.

Katya and Maddox took the stairs two at a time up to the sixth floor.

Maddox slowed near the top to wait for Katya. Adrenaline pulsed through his veins at the prospect of breaking and entering someone's apartment. He'd always lived his life by following the rules. This was outside his comfort zone, but it had to be done. They needed to know how the weapons got into Katya's apartment. Maddox was almost certain the furniture delivery was the key.

"Casey said it was a red leather sofa and a matching

love seat," Katya reminded him as they paused in the stairwell.

With a nod, Maddox pushed through the stairwell door and hurried down the hallway to apartment 627.

He pressed his ear to the door and listened. Nothing. No sounds of movement, voices or music. After taking a deep breath, he slid the master key card Casey had provided into the door lock and waited for it to give him a green light. The locking mechanism clicked and the light blinked green.

As soon as the door swung open, Maddox and Katya rushed inside, closing the door behind them to keep other tenants from looking in while they poked around.

The red leather sofa sat against the living room wall, the love seat stood with its back to the entrance, framing the living area.

Without saying a word, Maddox and Katya rushed to the furniture and pulled the cushions from the seats. Beneath the cushions both pieces looked like most sofas, with a layer of fabric and padding beneath.

"Grab the other end," Maddox said, grasping the end of the couch. Together, they tipped the couch over. Again, nothing looked like a storage place for weapons.

"How did they do it?" Katya voiced the question in Maddox's mind.

"I don't know."

"Should we check out my apartment? It's the one right below this one."

Maddox shook his head. "If the cops or the FBI are looking for you, they might have someone watching it."

"They would watch the building entrances, too. We succeeded in making it this far…"

For a moment Maddox considered her argument.

"We are in danger no matter where we go," Katya continued. "Besides, we might find a clue as to how they got the weapons in without detection."

"Okay, but I go first."

"As they say in the American movies…" Katya stuck out her hand for him to shake. "Deal."

"Deal." He took her hand, pulled her to him and kissed her. Then he headed for the stairwell.

On the fifth floor, Maddox scanned the hallway before edging out. "Stay here until I tell you to come," he said to Katya.

Yellow crime-scene tape crisscrossed apartment 527. Maddox carefully removed one end of the wide ribbon, shoved the key in the lock and pushed the door open.

He slipped through the doorway, into the apartment. Tastefully furnished with solid mahogany occasional tables and a soft, cream leather sofa festooned with colorful cushions in shades of burgundy, pumpkin and apple green, the room should have been warm and inviting. But the place was a wreck. Kitchen cabinet doors hung open, dishes and canned goods littered the polished granite counters. In the bedroom, drawers were laid across the dresser top and bed, their contents tossed.

"They took my photograph," a soft voice whispered behind him.

Maddox spun to face Katya. "I thought I told you to stay put."

"Someone was coming up the stairs. I had to move or be discovered."

Although he didn't want to, Maddox accepted her

explanation. "See anything out of place, missing or different?"

"Other than the fact they went through all my belongings and made a mess?" She sighed. "I do not know." Katya reached for the drawer containing her panties, her face reddening. "It's hard to accept that people have gone through my personal belongings." She glanced around the bedroom and out toward the living area. "Where are the crates of weapons they say I had?"

"The FBI or ATF must have confiscated them as evidence." He didn't know what he'd expected by sneaking into her apartment, but the effort had netted nothing.

Katya released the undergarment she held and crossed to the nightstand, her fingers brushing its surface. "They even took the photograph of my father and brother." She hugged her arms around her middle. "It was the only one I brought with me to America. I feel as if I have been violated." Her gaze shifted to his, her ice-blue eyes suspiciously bright, the dark smudges beneath them more noticeable.

"To be expected when strangers go through your stuff." Maddox wanted to go to her, wrap her in his arms and drive away the fear and sadness. If he did, he wasn't sure he could let go again or stay alert and focus on keeping them alive.

On the dresser, Maddox found a gold-plated hairbrush and let his finger trace the intricate design on its back. "Is this some kind of coat of arms?"

Katya stiffened. "Why do you ask?"

"It's the same as the one on your pendant. Does it have special meaning?"

"The pendant and the brush were gifts from my father. The symbol is our family crest."

"It looks expensive. This apartment looks expensive." Maddox stared around again with a more critical eye. "What did you say your father did?"

She turned away and headed for the living room. "He was an important political figure in my country. Should we get out of here before someone comes looking for me?"

Maddox followed her out of the room. "I suspect you're still not telling me the entire truth."

"Oh, it is true. My father was an important political figure in Trejikistan."

His gut told him there was more to it than that. "He wasn't a terrorist, was he?"

Katya rounded on him, the color flaring in her cheeks. "My father was an honorable man, concerned only with his people—the people of Trejikistan. He would never kill innocents or destroy out of hatred. He was good and kind and respected—"

Maddox grabbed her arms and held her still. "Okay, okay. Your father wasn't a terrorist." He stared down into her eyes, a moment before full of sadness, now flashing with the fire of her passion. How he'd love to make love to her and see her eyes flare with another kind of passion.

Despite their need to hurry, to get out of the apartment building before they were caught, Maddox couldn't stop himself from stealing a kiss.

Just one.

His mouth descended on hers, hard and swift.

Still stiff, she resisted his caress.

Maddox softened his assault, teasing the line of her lips with his tongue, urging her to open and let him in.

A little at a time, her shoulders relaxed, and finally, with a soft sigh, she unclenched her teeth.

He swept in, his tongue tasting, thrusting and ravaging her. She spread her hands across his chest, her fingers digging into his shirt. She stood on her toes, leaning into him, their bodies melting together.

He was the first to break away, but only far enough to trail kisses across her cheek, to take her earlobe between his teeth. "You make me ache."

Her gentle laugh made him even hotter. "I do not know whether to apologize or to be flattered."

"Both. I can't think when you're in the same room. Given the situation, that could be dangerous." He moved her away from him, sucking in a deep breath. "Much as I'd like to continue this conversation, we should get down to the control room and see what Casey has found."

"Agreed." She touched her fingers to her swollen lips and ducked past him into the hallway.

They took the stairs back down to the main level and emerged into the hallway near the door to the control room.

Casey opened it before they could knock. "I saw you coming. Come see what I found." He let them in, looked out toward the lobby and then locked the door. "I was able to bring up the day of the raid by the ATF."

The room contained an elaborate array of screens. Each revealed different floors and community spaces in the building, even exterior corners and the lobby.

Maddox's pulse quickened. "Did you figure out how they got the weapons in?"

Casey's lips twisted. "Yes and no."

A surge of impatience made Maddox want to shake

the security guard. "What do you mean, *yes and no?*" His words came out angrier than he'd intended.

Katya stepped between the two men. "Casey, show us what you have."

The young man sat at a computer keyboard separate from the other video screens, and clicked on a file. "Here. Watch this."

The video played, displaying an almost-empty lobby with the occasional tenant entering or leaving, the image slightly grainy, yet clear enough to make out the faces.

A man entered pushing a dolly with a large box, the size of a love seat. He disappeared from the camera's view onto the elevator.

A few minutes later, he exited the elevator with an empty dolly only to return a few minutes later with another box of a similar size to the first.

"Wasn't the sofa larger than that?" Katya asked.

"Yes." Maddox nodded, his gaze fixed to the screen and what happened next.

"Do you have the security video of the fifth floor about the time he would have gotten off the elevator?"

"I checked. This is the interesting part." Casey clicked another icon displaying the man with the box in the elevator. The man turned his back to the camera, partially out of sight, then a hand came up with a spray can and suddenly the video turned black.

"Where did the picture go?"

"That's the interesting part. I think he used black spray paint. Now listen." Casey increased the volume.

The automated assistant for the elevator sang out, *Fifth floor.* A swishing was then followed by the rumble of a heavy cart bumping over the elevator threshold.

"Fifth, not sixth floor," Katya said.

"And an extra love seat," Casey added. "I was on the phone at that time and didn't catch the additional load."

"Back it up." Maddox leaned forward.

Casey rewound the video to the where the man on the elevator faced the camera.

Maddox poked a finger at the screen. "Stop."

The frame stopped on the man's face, giving a fairly clear picture of him. Blond hair, gray or blue eyes, tall with a muscular build under the gray coveralls of a delivery driver.

"I need you to send a copy of that picture to an email address."

As Casey brought up his email account, Maddox wrote an address on a sticky note pad. "Send it there."

The young security guard keyed in the email address. Just as he maneuvered his mouse and clicked the Send button, Katya gasped.

"Boys, we have company." She pointed at the screen displaying the lobby. Men dressed in blue coveralls emblazoned with the bold yellow letters ATF AGENT entered, carrying scary-looking automatic weapons.

Chapter Fourteen

Katya's heart thundered in her chest like a bass drummer out of control. "Is there another way out of here?" she turned around looking for a back exit, anywhere she could go to escape the law enforcement officials who'd obviously been tipped off by someone.

"No, that's it." Casey nodded toward the door, then his eyes widened and a grin spread across his face. "Wait." He jumped up from his chair and ran across the small control room to the back wall. "If I recall correctly from my orientation, we have an emergency exit somewhere around here, just for the building security force that leads from the back of the control room to the parking garage two floors down." Like a madman, he pushed aside boxes and a copy machine, revealing a small door in the back wall. "I never think about it because we aren't supposed to use it unless it's a real emergency. I, personally, have never actually been down there."

He fumbled with the keys on his massive keychain, fitting one at a time into the door's lock. "Geez, which one of these keys goes to the door? I've never opened the door so I really don't know which one will make it open—*if* I even have the key."

Katya alternated between monitoring the screen and the progress the ATF men were making toward the control room and checking on Casey's progress in the back of the room. "Hurry, Casey. Some of them are headed up the elevator. Two are on their way here."

"I'm going as fast as I can." Casey dropped the ring of keys on the floor and dove to recover. "How close are they now?"

"Outside the door to the control room," Katya said, her voice low. With her insides quaking, she abandoned the screen and ran for the little door.

As she reached the two men standing there, Casey fitted a key in the lock and turned it. The door opened to reveal a metal ladder leading down a tiny shaft into darkness.

"Wow, this is too cool." Casey stared down at the escape route and then stepped aside, motioning for them to proceed. "You two better go."

Katya almost backed away. Dark, narrow ladders into an abyss weren't a normal, everyday occurrence in her life.

Maddox stepped up to the door. "I'll go first." He cupped her cheek. "I'll be there—all you have to do is follow my voice." He pressed his lips to hers in a hasty kiss. "Ready?"

She nodded and waited.

Maddox climbed onto the ladder and lowered himself into the darkness. "Now you, Katya. It's not so bad once you start down."

Katya, her hands shaking, grasped the cold metal rungs and placed her feet on the first step.

A loud banging on the control room door made her jerk and almost lose her hold on the ladder.

"Go," Casey whispered. "I have to shut the door and move the boxes in place before I let the ATF in. Be careful."

"Thanks, Casey. For everything." Katya sucked in a deep breath and lowered herself down the rungs.

Above her, Casey closed the door, shutting out all the light, leaving her in utter darkness.

"It's okay, Katya," Maddox said below her. He touched her foot. "One step at a time, and we'll get out of this."

Katya clung to the ladder, her breathing coming in quick, shallow pants, her fingers in a death grip on the metal rung. "I can't do this."

"Yes, you can." He stroked her calf then guided her foot to the next step. "See? One at a time."

"I am beginning to think this nightmare will never end."

"It will. Keep moving." Maddox coaxed and guided her every step of the way.

After what seemed like forever, dull gray light shone up the shaft from the bottom. Then Maddox was dropping the last few steps into a secluded area in the parking garage. He held his arms up. "You have to jump from the last rung. It's only five feet down. I'll catch you."

Katya climbed as low as she could, then let go, falling the last five feet into Maddox's arms. For a long moment, he held her, smoothing his hands over her hair. She wished she could stay that way forever, in the warmth and security of Maddox Thunder Horse's arms. She looked up into his face. "Do you make it a habit of saving damsels in distress?"

Maddox's expression hardened, his jaw tightening.

"No. Sometimes I'm too late." His arms dropped to his sides and he turned away.

Katya remembered what his mother had said about Maddox's fiancée dying in a blizzard. "You have to let go of the past, Maddox. You did not kill your fiancée—the blizzard did."

"What do you know about it? You weren't there."

"No, and I was not there for my father when he was murdered." Katya touched Maddox's arm. "You do not know how I wished I had been there for him."

He turned on her. "And if you had, you'd be dead, too."

"Exactly. You do not know how many times over the past couple of days I wished I could die and be with him."

"But you didn't."

"I know." Her hand moved up his arm. "Because of you."

"I won't always be there."

"No, but I am thankful for when you are." She pressed her cheek to his chest and hugged him around his middle. "I know you will not always be there. Especially when I go back to my country." She hugged him hard, then pushed away. "But we have to get out of here, or I will never make it back."

Maddox grabbed her hand and stopped her from stepping out of the concrete alcove. "Would that be such a bad thing?"

She gazed back at him, wishing with all her heart that she didn't have to return to Trejikistan. If she had her choice, she would stay with this tall, dark Lakota native on the Plains of North Dakota with his beloved wild horses. What a glorious life that would be. "Yes, I have to return to my country."

Maddox nodded and, still holding her hand, stepped up to the corner of the alcove, peering around the edge.

Nothing moved in the garage, the spaces empty, most of the tenants gone to work for the day.

Maddox tugged her hand, drawing her along the walls, keeping to the shadows. When they reached the exit, Katya yanked Maddox back.

A big, black van stood in the road, against the curb. Several men in the navy blue uniforms of the ATF team stood beside it, talking into handheld radios.

Maddox pointed to a bush close to the exit ramp. He let go of her hand, his gaze on the men by the van, then he ran across the ramp and dove into the bush.

The men at the van continued to talk on their handheld radios, oblivious to Maddox's exit.

Her heart thumping in her chest, Katya focused on the men in the street. When she was sure they were not looking, she followed Maddox, running across the concrete ramp. She dove behind the bushes, crashing into Maddox. He caught her and cushioned her fall, pressing a finger to her lips.

He parted the bushes and stared out.

Katya held her breath. Would this be it? Would the ATF finally catch up with their suspected terrorist?

What appeared to be the man in charge spoke to several men standing in front of him and pointed toward the building, specifically the garage exit.

"Time to move out." Ducking low, Maddox pushed between the bushes and the brick wall of the parking garage until they reached the far corner, leading toward the next building. A small gap between the hedges was all that separated the buildings.

Maddox went first, then Katya.

Someone shouted behind them.

Katya and Maddox didn't look back. They ran down a side street, leaving the apartment complex and the ATF behind.

Maddox didn't stop until they were ten blocks away. He yanked Katya behind a building and they both bent over at the middle, gasping for air.

Katya couldn't get enough oxygen. She dropped to her knees, her head thrown back, pulling in air as fast as her lungs could take it. "What…do…we…do now?"

Maddox straightened, his chest heaving, but closer to normal than Katya felt. "I had Casey send that picture to my brother, Pierce. He's an FBI agent. Maybe he can identify the man."

"In the meantime, what else can I do? I don't have anywhere to go, no one who can clear me." Her lungs hurt, her shins and calves screamed from the effort she'd expended.

"We locate a place to hole up until we hear from Pierce." Maddox looked around. "We should be able to find a motel around here."

"A motel?" she asked, her shoulders drooping. She didn't think she could run another step.

Maddox glanced at her. "We need rest."

Katya nodded, the idea of a pillow and a comfortable bed so very appealing after being on the road all night and chased by a crazed killer and the ATF. "A motel sounds great. Will it be safe?"

"As safe as anything when you consider that the ATF is after you."

She grimaced at Maddox. "You are making me feel *so* much better."

He smiled and held out his hand. "Good, then let's get moving. We aren't out of hot water yet."

She laid her hand in his and let him pull her to her feet and into his arms. "Hot water sounds wonderful. I could use a bath."

Katya guided them to a bus stop with a route to the outskirts of Minneapolis. Keeping her head down, Katya climbed aboard and moved to a backseat where she pressed her hand to her face, pretending to cough. Maddox sat beside her, shielding her from view of the other passengers. He didn't like being in a public place where someone might recognize her.

Maddox found a motel off the beaten path of the interstates and main thoroughfares. While he obtained a key, Katya huddled in the bushes at the far end of the parking lot.

He didn't like leaving her even for a moment, but he couldn't risk a clerk matching her face to the ones plastered all over the television screen behind him.

He'd asked for a room at the end of the building, farthest away from the road, and paid cash. When he unlocked the door, he scanned the parking lot and the street beyond before he motioned for Katya to join him.

Keeping close to the hedges surrounding the parking lot, she moved quickly and quietly until she entered the room.

Maddox shut the door and locked the dead bolt. "Well, now that wasn't so bad, was it?"

Katya unzipped her heavy winter coat and dropped it onto a chair. She stood with her shoulders sagging, and stripped the hat from her head, her long luscious locks falling free in a tangled mess around her face. Her pale face was as pale as when he'd first found her almost dead by a frozen river. The dark smudges beneath her eyes stood out like bruises. Yet, despite how tired and worn out she looked, she was still the most beautiful woman Maddox had ever seen.

"I'm tired," she laughed, her voice shaky, her lips trembling.

"I'll bet." He held out his arms and she fell into them.

For a long moment, they stayed that way, holding each other, the warmth of her body chasing away the chill in Maddox's. A chill that went back to the day Susan died in his arms. She was right. He couldn't hold onto the past, not when the present was kicking his butt.

"You can have the bathroom first."

"Thanks. But I don't think I can move." She sighed and leaned closer.

"I'd help, but I need to place a call to my brother, Pierce, and check on Tuck."

Katya stepped away, her arms dropping to her sides. "That's more important. I'll be quick."

As Katya stepped into the little bathroom, Maddox pulled the throwaway cell phone from his pocket and dialed Pierce's number.

"Pierce? Maddox here."

"Where the hell are you?"

"I can't tell you yet. Are you near a computer?"

"I can be, give me a sec."

A moment later Maddox heard the squeak of what had to be an office chair.

"Shoot, brother," Pierce said.

"I had an email sent to you. It contains a picture of

a man we think planted the weapons in Katya's room. He might also be the man who's been following her and tried to shoot her."

"I'm on it. I'll see what we can do to ID the guy. Can I reach you again at this number?"

"Yes."

"I'll call as soon as I get a hit on your man."

"The sooner the better. We're hiding out from just about every law enforcement agency in the country and this man you're going to be looking to match."

"I know. We even got the heads-up on the girl here at the Bureau. Won't be long before you're on the same dance card. Be safe."

"Will do." Maddox clicked the Off button and sighed. After another call home to make sure Tuck, Dante and his mother were all right, he let some of the tension slide from his shoulders. For the moment they were relatively safe.

The sound of the shower called to Maddox. Knowing that Katya was naked in it made the decision for him.

He stripped off his clothes and entered the bathroom, shoving aside the curtain.

Katya, her face and head beneath the water, rinsing the suds out of her eyes, didn't hear him enter.

God, she had a beautiful body. Maddox stepped into the tub behind her and slid his hands around her waist.

She jumped at first. When she realized who it was, she relaxed, leaning against him. Katya fit him perfectly.

He rubbed soap in his palms and smoothed them over her belly and upward to cup her breasts.

Katya breathed deeply, her chest pushing against his

hands. She reached behind her, capturing his buttocks, pressing him closer, his erection nudging against her.

He tweaked her nipples, drawing them to a hardened point. Then his fingers trailed through the slippery soap down her torso, over her flat abdomen to the thatch of curls at the apex of her thighs.

Her hand found his shaft behind her and stroked him from tip to stem.

Maddox groaned, his fingers dipping into her folds, matching the rhythm of her strokes, flicking and teasing her until her back arched against him.

He wouldn't last long, not as hot as she made him and as good as her body felt against his. Nothing could top that, except being inside her.

As if reading his thoughts, Katya turned in his arms, one perfect leg trailing up over his calf.

He hooked her thighs in his hands and turned her back to the cool hard tile wall of the shower, balancing her as he lowered her down until he nudged at her opening.

"Please," she said, easing herself down until she took him fully inside.

Maddox's breath caught in his throat. "You feel so good."

"Make love to me, Maddox, like this is the last time."

He froze, his hands holding her legs wrapped around his waist. "No. I'll make love to you like this is the first time." He drove into her. "The first of many." In and out, he thrust, the tension pulsing through his body. Desperation, frustration and anger fueled his passion, pushing him harder and faster.

Katya had come to mean more to him than he ever

expected, and he didn't want to lose her—wouldn't lose her. Not after all they had been through together.

When he climaxed, he pulled her close, holding her tight against his body.

Her arms and legs clung to him, her body shaking. They remained this way until their passion and the water cooled.

Maddox set Katya on her feet and they finished rinsing off. He dried her body and she dried his. Maddox carried Katya to the bed, laying her among the sheets, where he kissed every inch of her body. When she tried to return the gesture, he stopped her. "No, I want you to sleep. This is my treat."

Katya lay back, her damp curls splayed out across the pillow, while Maddox explored every inch of her body with his lips. She fell asleep soon after.

Although he could have gone for another round of lovemaking, he knew she was tired and his mind and muscles ached for sleep. Eventually, he crawled beside her and fell into a deep sleep, her body curled against him. Where she belonged.

He couldn't have been asleep for long when his cell phone buzzed on the nightstand beside the bed. Maddox fumbled for the phone, punching at the unfamiliar buttons until he stopped the ringing. "Yeah."

"Maddox, you have a serious problem."

It took him a moment to surface from sleepiness to recognize his brother Pierce's voice. He shoved a hand through his hair and sat up, hoping the movement would jar him more fully awake. "What problem?"

"The man who is after Katya is a professional assassin."

Chapter Fifteen

"What is it?" Katya sat up behind him, pressing her naked breasts against Maddox's back.

He sucked in a deep breath, completely awake, adrenaline firing throughout his system. "Who is he and who would have hired him?"

"Richard Fulton, alias, Rick Masters, alias, Patrick Delaney, and the aliases go on. We suspect him of at least twenty assassinations and those are only the ones we know about. He's at the top of the FBI's Most Wanted List."

"Damn." Maddox sat back, sick to his stomach. "What do we do?"

"You can't keep her safe by yourself," Pierce said. "You need to let me help."

"I can't drag you into this. I've already implicated the rest of the family in Katya's problem—no need to drag you in as well."

"Just my knowledge of this has me fully involved. Let us help. We have the resources to figure this thing out."

"The ATF hasn't figured it out yet. How can the FBI?"

"I have a vested interest, brother," Pierce's voice

dropped, low and insistent. "I can get my boss to buy in. We bring in the girl, Fulton will follow."

"Use her as bait?"

"No, provide her protection."

"The way this guy has followed us, he'll find her."

"Not where we'll hide her. We can set her up in a safe house with dedicated agents to guard her. Then we can set up a phony safe house and let it slip that she's there. He'll come after her, we'll get our man and Katya will be cleared."

"Sounds like you have this all planned out."

"Either way, Maddox, she's not safe out on her own."

"She has me and she's still alive."

"Fulton is a professional. He always gets his mark. It's only a matter of time."

Maddox held the phone to his ear, but he didn't respond. "Let me think about it. I'll call you back."

"Maddox—" Pierce shouted into the phone as Maddox hit the Off button.

Let someone else protect Katya? Every one of Maddox's brain cells screamed, *No!* But he wasn't alone in this. Katya had a say in what she wanted to do.

"I only caught a little of that." Katya pulled the sheet up over her trembling body, her eyes rounded. "An assassin?" She shook hard, her fingers clenching the sheet to her breasts.

"Richard Fulton." Maddox ran his hand through his hair. "From what Pierce said, the man is a paid assassin and extremely dangerous. He's on the top of the FBI's Most Wanted List."

"What did your brother suggest?"

Maddox stared across at her, his chest tightening. "He

wants to put you in a safe house and use you as bait to catch Fulton."

Katya didn't utter a sound, the only indication that she heard him was a slight widening of her already rounded blue eyes.

"My gut feeling on this is no." Maddox twisted the phone in one hand. "We've managed to stay safe this long, we can continue doing what we've been doing while the FBI looks into the video we sent."

"How long will it take for them to clear me of suspicion?"

"I don't know."

"I don't have time to wait for a full-fledged investigation." She dropped the sheet and crawled across the bed to Maddox where she kneeled beside him. "I can't expect you to protect me forever."

He frowned and opened his mouth to protest, but she placed a finger over his lips and then replaced it with her mouth. She brushed a kiss across his lips and pressed her cheek to his. "I want to go to the safe house, Maddox. But I want it on the condition that I am freed of charges and sent back to Trejikistan once they capture the assassin."

He slipped his hands around her waist and pulled her onto his lap. "What if I can't let you go?"

"You have to. I am not your responsibility and no matter how this ends, I cannot stay." She reached up and cupped his cheeks with her hands. "I have to go home."

Maddox stared down into her eyes. Anger, fear and something else battled in his heart, making his chest hurt. He captured her hands in his and squeezed them hard. "If that's the way you want it." He stood, lifting her with him to set her on the floor.

As much as he wanted to drag her naked body back to the bed, he didn't. She wanted to leave, and he'd make it possible. As she'd stated from the very beginning, back in the cave on the ranch, *no strings.* "Get dressed. I'll arrange a transfer point with the FBI." Too bad the strings he'd allowed to grow were now choking his heart.

HOURS LATER, KAT STOOD at the window, staring out at the group of cars leaving the small house perched in an isolated location west of Minneapolis. Maddox had left well over an hour ago after he had seen her settled in. He had not wanted to go, but she insisted. Better to cut the ties now. If all went as planned, she would be back in her country within the week.

The four men positioned at every corner remained outside.

"You should be safe here." Pierce Thunder Horse laid a hand on her shoulder. "We've leaked word that you are at the other safe house. We have an entire squad of agents surrounding it, ready to capture Fulton as soon as he makes his move."

Katya didn't respond, her gaze on the now empty road.

Pierce's lips tipped into a small smile. "Maddox didn't look too happy about leaving you with me. What's up between you two?"

"Nothing," she replied. Her life was back in Trejikistan. Her people needed her leadership to see them through the next few months in preparation for their first election. Maddox had a family and a ranch to go home to. She had a country to lead into democracy.

"If it makes you feel any better, Maddox looked pretty miserable."

Why did Maddox's brother insist on poking at her wounds? She frowned and captured Pierce's gaze in his reflection in the window. "Why would that make me feel better?"

"He made me promise to take good care of you."

"He would do that for anyone. Maddox is a good man."

"True." Pierce nodded. "But he seems a little hurt that you chose the FBI to look after you rather than him."

"I do not know why. I have only been trouble to him since he saved me out in the canyon."

Pierce chuckled. "Yeah, I heard about some of that from Tuck. I didn't think you'd come to the FBI for help. What changed your mind?"

Katya avoided Pierce's gaze in the window's reflection, preferring to stare out at the dirt road leading to the remote cabin. "Maddox."

"He did? Maddox convinced you to turn yourself over to us?"

"No. I did it for Maddox. I could not continue to lead him on."

"How so?"

"I have to return to Trejikistan." She straightened her shoulders the way her mother had taught her so long ago. *You are royalty. Act like it.* "It is my duty."

"And he didn't want you to go?"

She nodded.

"Did you tell him why you had to return?"

"No." She hadn't wanted anything to change between them. Had he known who she was, he might have been like everyone else and looked at her differently, like a freak or someone who was too fragile to even think for herself.

"Did you tell him about your family?" Pierce persisted.

Katya's heart skipped a beat and she turned to face Maddox's brother. "What do you know about my family?"

"I just got your dossier on my way out the door to pick you up." He held a file in his hands and flipped it open. "Seems your full name is Princess Alexi Katya Ivanov. Daughter of the late Boris Ivanov, king of Trejikistan."

She sucked in a deep breath and let it out slowly. "Did you tell Maddox?"

"I didn't have time to read the dossier until we were on our way out here."

"Don't tell him, please." She knew she had to leave, and she didn't want Maddox's opinion or memories of her to change because of a stupid title that would mean nothing in a few months.

"Why not?"

"I came to America to be me, not Princess Alexi Katya Ivanov. If Maddox chooses to remember me, I would prefer him to remember me as just a girl, a foreign exchange student, not a princess from some faraway land few people in America had even heard of." She took Pierce's hands in hers. "Please, don't tell him."

Pierce stared down into her eyes. "I'm beginning to see why Maddox has fallen in love with you."

Katya shook her head, her hands falling to her sides. "Do not be foolish. We have not known each other long enough for him to fall in love with me."

"He left for home with the most wounded-dog look

on his face I've seen in a long time. What else could it be?"

"Not love." Katya turned to stare out the window again.

Pierce started to say something else when his cell phone rang. "Excuse me." He turned and walked into the kitchen of the little cabin.

Katya strained to hear his end of the conversation.

"You bastard, what have you done with my brother?" Pierce's expletive drew Katya into the kitchen, his privacy be damned.

Her pulse thundered in every vein, her heart banging against her chest. Maddox was in trouble.

Pierce paced the length of the small kitchen, the phone pressed to his ear with one hand, the other clenched in a tight fist by his side. "Where do you want to make the transfer?"

Katya's fingers twisted together and she bit down hard on her lip to keep it from trembling. What had happened to Maddox?

Pierce hit the Off button and reared back to throw the phone against the wall.

Katya caught his arm before he could let the device fly. "What happened to Maddox?"

"Fulton has him and wants to make a trade. We're to meet him at a warehouse close to the Port of St. Paul in an hour."

"He wants to trade me for Maddox?"

Pierce looked at her, his mouth set in a firm line. "Yeah. But I can't do that."

Katya nodded, every part of her body growing still. She knew what had to be done and didn't hesitate. "Yes, you can. We have to make the deal."

MADDOX PRESSED THE accelerator to the floor, pushing the rental car to its limit on the interstate between Minneapolis and Fargo. His little throwaway cell phone hadn't had reception since he left the Twin Cities.

The urge to turn around and go back fought with reason. He couldn't just go back to Minneapolis, find Katya and take her back under his wing. He wanted to force her to stay with him, even after all the danger died down. Thank God he'd insisted on taking her to the safe house himself. At least he knew how to find her.

What if Katya didn't want him to come?

She'd insisted that he leave her with the FBI. They knew better how to protect her. They were trained to man a safe house and provide the security needed to keep her out of Richard Fulton's sights. For all intents and purposes, *she* had rejected *him*. She had told him to leave.

Maddox had traveled nearly an hour away from the safe house before his resolve crumbled. He lifted his cell phone for the fifth time in as many minutes. Still no reception. Resisting the urge to throw the phone, he noticed an off ramp coming up. On this long stretch of interstate in Minnesota, they were few and far between. His foot slipped off the accelerator and the car veered off the road and onto the ramp. Maybe if he got to higher ground off the ramp he'd get a bar or two of reception.

He drove to the top of the ramp. The longer he was out of cell phone range, the more certain he was that something was wrong. He had to get hold of Pierce, even if it meant turning around and heading back to Minneapolis.

He checked his phone again. Still no bars. That

decided it. Without slowing, he barreled through the stop sign and flew across the overpass and onto the interstate, headed back east to Minneapolis. The sooner he was within range of a decent cell tower, the better. Once he talked to Pierce, he'd relax and return to the ranch.

As he neared Minneapolis and the turnoff to the safe house, four bars sprang up on his cell phone screen. Finally! He hit the speed-dial button for his brother and immediately got his answering machine. An hour out and just under an hour back since he'd left Katya and his brother at the safe house. Why he didn't trust them to keep Katya safe, he didn't know. But he couldn't just walk away. Not after the past two days of taking care of her. If something happened...

He tried his brother again. Still no answer.

Damn! Why wasn't he responding? A lump of lead weighed heavily in his gut. Was the safe house outside cell phone reception? Or could it be that Katya was once again in trouble?.

"MADDOX WOULDN'T WANT you to do this." Pierce held the door for Katya to climb into the SUV that would carry her to the warehouses located on the St. Paul side of the Mississippi River.

"Maddox cannot speak for himself. Because of me, he is a hostage of that murdering bastard." Katya stared straight ahead, calm, determined to face whatever lay ahead. Maddox had rescued her several times over the past couple days. If it was the last thing she did, she would make sure he came out of this fiasco alive.

Images of him holding her close in the sleeping bag in the cave kept playing through her mind. The dark

Native American with his long, straight black hair had hands that could crush, but were gentle. He had coaxed her away from a frozen death, given her a second chance to redeem her name, her country and her life. The least she could do was negotiate his freedom.

"I have a squad of agents moving into place around the warehouse. If Fulton shows, they'll nab him. Maybe even before you arrive."

She touched Pierce's arm. "No! You cannot let Fulton see them. If he suspects we are not alone, he might hurt Maddox."

"Don't worry. They are under strict instructions not to make a move until they know where Maddox is and have a clear shot at Fulton."

Bullets might fly and one might hit Maddox. "Can we just trade me for Maddox and leave all the bullets in the guns?"

Pierce smiled at her. "You really like the guy, don't you?"

She nodded. "He is a good man. He does not deserve to be caught in the cross fire."

"I agree. But we have to take Fulton out or you'll never be safe."

"I don't care about me."

"Consider that his next victim will not be safe."

"You're right."

Pierce dug a small disc out of his shirt pocket and handed it to her. "Put this in a pocket, somewhere that can't be found. A safe place where you won't lose it."

She turned the disc over. A plain shiny disc, it looked like a large watch battery. "What is it?"

"A gift from me and Maddox. In case things don't go according to plan."

She shrugged and shoved the disc into her pocket.

"No, someplace no one would think to look."

Katya's brows pulled together. "Is this a GPS tracking device?"

Pierce grinned. "Smart as well as beautiful. Yes. That's exactly what it is. Just in case we get separated, we'll be able to find you."

She pulled the disc from her pocket and pulled the neckline of her sweater out enough so she could slide the disc into her bra. "Better?"

"Much." Pierce gulped. "Definitely smart as well as beautiful. Eyes on the road, Thunder Horse," he said beneath his breath.

The sedan in front of them slowed as they neared a T-intersection, crowded by trees and tall mounds of snow that had been pushed off the road.

As the car moved out into the road, a truck barreled at it from the south, slamming into the side of the sedan, sending it careening off the road and into a ditch.

Katya screamed.

The SUV driver slammed on the brakes and Katya hit the seat back in front of her, stunning her.

Before she knew what was happening her door jerked open and she was yanked from the SUV, a gun pointed at her head. "Don't try anything or I'll kill her," a deep male voice demanded.

"You kill her and you're a dead man." Pierce held his gun up in his hand, letting it dangle from the trigger guard. "Let the girl go."

"No can do. She's money."

"What have you done with Maddox?"

Fulton laughed. "Nothing. Not a damn thing. He's probably halfway to North Dakota by now. Move it,

Princess, we have an appointment to make." He grabbed her elbow and backed away from the vehicle, the gun pressing into her temple.

Despite the threat to her life, Katya couldn't stop the flood of relief from warming her insides. Maddox was safe. Fulton hadn't captured him.

The metal gun barrel bounced, slamming into her temple as Fulton forced her to walk backwards to the waiting truck with the smashed front end. The assassin slid into the driver's seat, pulling her in next to him, close enough that if anyone tried to shoot at them, they'd hit her as well. "Close the door."

Katya reached for the handle and pulled the door toward her. All the while Fulton kept his head close to hers, using her as a human shield.

He shifted the gun to his left hand and reached for the gearshift with his right. "Don't get any ideas. I can shoot equally well with both hands." With a quick tug, he had it in reverse, backing away from the FBI vehicles until they were out of range. Then he swung the truck around and hit the accelerator, rocketing the vehicle down the highway.

Katya let him take her without a fight. She wanted to get as far away from the agents as possible. Enough people had been hurt in this man's quest to capture her. This way Maddox's brother, Pierce, would be safe.

"You're a hired assassin, aren't you?" Katya asked.

"Not your business."

"When I'm the target, that makes it my business," she retorted.

Fulton laughed, driving one-handed. "The princess has a mouth on her."

"Who hired you to kill me?"

The man focused on navigating the road ahead. "Who said I was going to kill you?"

"You've shot enough bullets at me to take me out a couple times."

"If I'd wanted to hit you, trust me, I'd have hit you."

"You didn't answer me." She tried to turn her head to look at him, but he held the gun to her temple, pressing so hard she couldn't. "Who hired you?"

"Your future husband."

"What?" She tried again to turn her head. Cold, hard metal dug into her flesh. "What do you mean, my future husband?"

"You're a smart girl, figure it out." He slowed to negotiate a turn from the county road to a state highway. The truck shot forward, slipping sideways on a patch of ice.

Katya shook her head. "I don't have a future husband."

"You do now, and he was willing to pay big bucks for me to bring you back to Trejikistan to marry him."

"Trejikistan?" She searched her memory for anyone who had ever even hinted at wanting to marry her back in her country. She'd eavesdropped on a conversation between her father and... "Vladimir?"

"Bingo! Give the princess a prize."

"Vladimir wants to marry me? Why?"

"You're failing in my estimation, Princess, and I was beginning to think you were a smart cookie." Her captor shook his head. "The man thinks that by marrying you, he can build his case as the new ruler now that your father is out of the way."

Katya gasped. "Vladimir is responsible for my father's death?"

"Not for me to say—you'll have to ask him. I don't like to brag about my work." His eyes narrowed, the gun pressing harder into her temple. "You've slipped through my fingers too often lately. Makes me look bad."

Rage boiled up inside her. This man had killed her father. "You murdering bastard. You can rot in hell for all the people you've murdered, and for what? A few dollars?"

"More than a few."

Katya stared at the road ahead, her blood pounding in her veins. She wanted to kill this man who'd taken her father from her, to make him hurt as much as he'd hurt her father and her family. "You're a coward, a lowlife murderer. You'll pay for this. I promise you."

"You need to shut up." He swerved, flinging her head against the window.

Katya blinked back the pain, refusing to show this man an ounce of fear. "How much is he paying you?"

"Enough. More if I bring you back alive. That's the beauty of it. I get paid either way. Dead or alive."

"If it's all the same to you. I'd prefer to be dead than to marry Vladimir." She grabbed the steering wheel and yanked it to the left.

Richard Fulton jammed his foot on the brakes, let go of the gun and used both hands to regain control of the vehicle. The truck veered off the road and into the ditch filled with mounds of snow.

Katya shoved the door open, jumped out and ran.

"Damn woman. Stop!" Footsteps pounded on the ground behind her.

She didn't look back, pushing harder to reach the

road. She had to get away from this killer and warn her country about Vladimir's plan. As she reached the top of the ditch, her feet slipped out from under her on a patch of ice and she went down hard, her head hitting the pavement.

Richard Fulton stood over her, his gun pointed at her head. "I should have killed you back in that canyon."

Blackness consumed her.

Chapter Sixteen

Maddox took the turn, skidding sideways and almost running into an SUV that barreled into the intersection—the SUV that had taken Katya to the safe house. What was it doing out here?

He blocked the road with his rental car and leaped out.

Pierce dropped down from the driver's seat and ran toward Maddox. "Fulton has her."

Maddox ground to a halt, all the air leaving his lungs in a rush as though he'd been sucker punched. "What?"

"Fulton set up an ambush and grabbed Katya before we realized what was happening." Pierce jerked his head toward the other agent who'd been in the SUV with him. "Move the car." He grabbed Maddox's arm. "Ride with us. We have a tracking device on her. He won't get far with her."

"If he doesn't kill her first." Maddox stated, his feet like lead as he forced himself to move toward the vehicle. He couldn't bear to find her dead. He'd been through that once with Susan.

"She's not dead. He'd have killed her on the spot, not taken her hostage. Hell, he'd have killed her a long time ago if he really wanted her dead. He's a paid assassin. They don't miss unless they want to."

Maddox climbed into the passenger seat of the SUV. Pierce climbed in beside him and tossed a device with a screen on it. "Follow the moving dot. That's Katya's tracking device."

"How did he find her? I thought safe houses were supposed to be secret."

"All we can figure is that he might have an insider in the FBI feeding him information."

"He knew where to find us when we were out at the hunting cabin." Maddox stared ahead as they pulled around the rental car and picked up the agent. "He knew where to find us in Medora. He was always there."

"It's as though he has his own tracking device on her."

"Her necklace," Maddox said. "Katya said her father gave it to her so that he'd always know she was safe. He must have had a tracking device embedded in it."

"And Fulton knew it. Someone from Katya's country had to have given him that information." Pierce shook his head. "She would never have been safe as long as she had that necklace on her. We should have taken all of her belongings away before we brought her to the safe house. Sorry, Maddox."

"She wouldn't have given it up easily." It was her last gift from her father. Maddox's teeth ground together at the thought of Katya in Fulton's hands. "The main thing is to get her back before Fulton does something stupid."

"That's the plan. I've mobilized a task force. They have the tracking device up on their screens and will converge on Fulton, wherever he takes her."

"As long as they don't hurt Katya."

"What, and start an international incident?" Pierce shot a look at Maddox. "I put out strict instructions not to harm a hair on her pretty head."

"Good." Maddox sat back, clenching and unclenching his fist. He'd feel a whole lot better when he saw Katya again. Alive. "They're headed for Minneapolis."

"We'll keep a safe distance from them until they come to a halt."

Minutes dragged by. Maddox's hands gripped the tracker, the knuckles growing whiter the longer they trailed the killer. What was happening to Katya? Was she still alive? The only thing they knew for certain was that she was with the killer. Would he never stop? "At what point will you try to force him off the road?"

"We won't. He'll have to stop sooner or later, if for nothing else, fuel. We follow until he does so."

"If we don't run out of gas before he does." Maddox stole a look at the gas gauge.

"Don't worry. We're full and there's a backup tank."

Maddox's attention returned to the tracker. "Wait. I think they've stopped." He leaned closer. Was it true? Yes. The dot on the screen had stopped.

"Where?"

Maddox zoomed in on the tracking device and gave Pierce the address.

"That's near the port. What's he doing there?"

"Wherever he thinks he's going, he's not taking Katya with him." Maddox stared ahead.

Pierce relayed the information to the other agents. They agreed to set up operations two blocks from the tracker location and move in on foot. When he got off the radio, he stared across at Maddox. "You need to stay with the SUV. I can't risk having a civilian involved if shots are fired."

"Like hell."

"Maddox, I need to concentrate on saving Katya. Not you."

"I can't sit back and do nothing."

"You damn sure can."

Maddox clenched his teeth to keep from saying anything else.

"Promise you won't interfere?" Pierce insisted.

He nodded.

Two blocks from Katya's GPS location, the vehicles pulled together. Pierce joined the team and weapons were distributed—everything from Sig Sauer pistols to high-powered rifles only sharpshooters would know how to use correctly.

Darkness had fallen, the streetlights casting beams of light out into the street and shadows consuming all else.

As soon as the team set off, Maddox counted to ten and followed. He had promised not to interfere, but he didn't promise not to follow. Wherever Katya was, he wanted to be.

"GET UP!" FULTON SHOOK HER until her teeth rattled and her eyes opened.

Pain sliced through the back of her head as she stared up at her captor. "Where are we?"

For an answer, he yanked her to her feet and shoved her ahead of him toward a dark building that looked like a warehouse. The place smelled of rank water and diesel fumes.

"Where are we going?" she whispered, so careful not to speak too loudly that her voice echoed in her head. Her feet caught on an old cardboard box and she fell flat on her chest, the wind knocked from her lungs.

"Get up!" Fulton grabbed her by her hair and jerked her to her feet.

She got up quickly, standing on her toes to loosen his pull on her hair. His unrelenting hold brought unwanted tears to her eyes. "Okay, okay. I am coming." She hurried to keep up, all the while feeling for the tracking device she'd stuffed in her bra. She couldn't feel the little metal disc. The more she patted her chest, the more desperate she became. If she didn't have the disc, Pierce and the FBI would never find her. She could be tossed on a ship, or left somewhere to die, while they scratched their heads and wondered where Fulton had taken her.

Fulton yanked on her arm, forcing her ahead of him.

"What is your hurry, anyway?" she asked.

"The sooner I get you on the boat, the sooner I get paid." He reached the end of the alley and crossed a street to another equally dreary warehouse that appeared as though it hadn't been used in a decade. Windows, high on the brick walls, gaped open like faces frozen in horror, the glass broken, shadowy darkness revealing nothing within.

"I'm going on a boat?"

"On a container ship. In a container."

Katya sucked in a deep breath in an attempt to ease the panic rising in her throat. "How much is my cousin paying you?"

"Shut up."

"He doesn't actually have access to any money in Trejikistan without my—or my brother's—permission. Did you know that?"

Fulton came to an abrupt halt and glared down at her. "You'd better hope he has the money he promised to pay. If not, you'll both die."

She waited until Fulton resumed his breakneck pace, knowing she had scored with her previous comment. Maybe she could get him so distracted that she could escape. "Did you know that my cousin is a habitual liar? He once promised to buy a yacht from an English duke, but after testing it for six months, he backed out of the deal, claiming it was damaged."

"Shut up, woman!" Fulton jerked her to a halt and slammed her up against a brick wall. "Your mouth will get you killed. One more comment, and I'm through messing with you."

Katya clamped her lips closed on her next retort. Fulton was distracted. Now she just had to look for an opportunity to trip him or pull free of his hold on her.

Her father's killer took off again, headed for the back of the vacant warehouse. They had to pass by a stack of broken pallets to get to the backdoor.

As they came alongside the pallets, Katya faked tripping, falling to her hands and knees.

"I should just shoot you now." He pointed his gun at her head, his breathing harsh and strained like a bull in a rage.

"Maybe you should," Katya taunted, her fingers closing around a single slat with nails protruding from the opposite end.

When he leaned forward to grab for her hair, she

stood up, swinging the board at the hand holding the weapon.

The nails jabbed into his wrist. Fulton screamed, flinging the gun to the ground.

"You bit—"

He didn't finish the word before Katya swung back around with the board, this time catching the side of his face. The nails dug into the skin and ripped a long bloody path across his cheek. He screamed again, grabbing for his face.

Katya flung the board at him and ran the other way as fast as she could. If she could only make it to the end of the building and duck down another alley, she might lose him.

Her heart raced, her breathing came in ragged gasps, but she pressed on, moving as fast as her feet would carry her in snow boots.

Feet pounded on the pavement behind her, sharp curses flung at her from the angry man. "When I catch you…"

She reached the corner and spun to the right, running all out. The buildings were too long to give her any cover or concealment. Her only hope was to outrun him. Given his height and athletic ability, that didn't seem likely. He'd brought her to the oldest warehouses imaginable. Most appeared abandoned. She was on her own, with no one to rescue her. If she planned to survive, she'd have to rescue herself.

She amazed herself when she rounded the end of the next building and ducked down a back alley. This one contained a rusty trash Dumpster and old metal barrels. Before Fulton appeared around the corner, Katya hid behind a barrel, as she searched the trash-strewn ground for something she could use as a weapon. She grabbed a broken beer bottle from the ground and held it in front of her as she peered between the barrels at the man moving toward her.

"You might as well come out," he said. "I'll find you sooner or later."

She kept still, her pulse banging so loudly against her eardrums she was afraid she wouldn't hear him when he made his next move.

"If you escape from me, I'll only go after your boyfriend," he taunted. "Do you want me to kill your boyfriend?"

Katya's breath caught in her throat. She wanted to jump out and stab the murderer in the face. He had killed her father, he had tried to kill her and Tuck, and now he was threatening Maddox. Enough was enough.

She tamped down her raging anger and waited until he stepped in front of the barrel behind which she hid. When he did, she leaped from her hiding place, screaming as loud as she could and thrusting the broken bottle into Fulton's face.

THE FBI TOOK THE direct route toward the blip on the GPS tracking screen. Maddox had seen the screen and had a general idea of the layout of the streets. He hoped to get close enough to Katya to be there if she needed him.

Maddox ran from building to building, working his way closer to the last blip he'd seen on the screen. Fulton had been moving Katya toward the river. Hopefully, he didn't plan to toss her in. Maddox didn't know whether or not Katya could swim. There were a lot of things he didn't know about Katya and, *dammit,* he wanted to find out. All he needed was a little more time with her.

A scream ripped through the night, firing his adrenaline. He ran in the direction of the sound, hoping it hadn't echoed off the buildings from the opposite direction. Running full tilt, he skidded around a corner and into an alley filled with trash, barrels and an abandoned Dumpster.

There among the debris were two shadowy figures struggling in the darkness.

"Katya!"

"Stay back or I'll kill her!" Fulton shouted, twisting his hands in her hair and yanking so hard, her feet left the ground.

Katya yelped and kicked out, landing a boot against his shins. "He isn't armed!" she yelled.

Maddox didn't slow down, didn't stop to think, his entire body in reaction mode to the danger Katya was in. He charged the two like a raging lion, roaring at the top of his lungs.

He hit Fulton on the side, flinging him up into the air. The man slammed into the heavy metal Dumpster, dragging Katya by the hair.

Thrown off balance, she hit the ground next to the assassin, but came up fighting, twisting and kicking.

As distracted by Katya as he was, Fulton didn't see Maddox's second advance until too late.

Maddox balled his fist and rammed it into the killer's face. Bones snapped and blood gushed from Fulton's nose.

Katya pulled free and flung herself out of the way.

The assassin pushed to his feet and lunged at Maddox,

hitting him in the gut. The two men fell to the ground, Fulton landing on top of Maddox.

Maddox bucked and fought to get his hands free, but remained pinned to the ground by the trained assassin. No matter how hard he tried, he couldn't shake free.

A loud crack rent the air and Fulton fell to the side, stunned.

Maddox leaped onto him and held him down.

Katya stood over the two men, holding a four-foot-long two-by-four like a warrior, ready to take on an entire army.

Suddenly the alley filled with men carrying weapons, one of them Pierce.

Momentarily distracted, Maddox wasn't prepared when Fulton rolled to the side and out from under him. The assassin leaped to his feet and ran.

Pierce and every other agent on the FBI assault team raced after him. He didn't get to the end of the warehouse building before Pierce caught up with him and slammed him to the ground in a flying tackle.

Four assault rifles pointed at the fugitive as Pierce yanked the man's hands behind his back and handcuffed him. "You have the right to remain silent…"

As Pierce read the man his rights, Maddox stood and looked around for Katya. More FBI special agents had arrived in the alley and Maddox couldn't find her among them. His heart skipped several beats. Panic made him push through the men standing around until he spotted the dark-haired woman, his chest tightening at the sight of her.

She sat on the pavement, her arms wrapped around her knees, her shoulders shaking. She looked like an abandoned child, her hair tousled, her face streaked with dirt. But she was the most beautiful woman Maddox had ever seen.

He sat beside her and pulled her into his arms. For a long moment, they leaned against each other.

Pressing his lips into her hair, he whispered, "Thanks for rescuing me."

She gave a shaky laugh and looked up into his face. "I should be thanking you."

The dark alley couldn't dim the light in her pale blue eyes. She smiled. "You're my hero."

"And you are mine. He had me until you came at him like a warrior." He smoothed the hair out of her face. "Where'd you learn to fight dirty like that?"

She cupped his face with her hand and leaned forward to brush a kiss across his lips. "I did what I had to." She kissed him again.

This time Maddox didn't let her off so lightly. His arms tightened around her and he deepened the kiss, his tongue pushing past her teeth to toy with hers.

She gave back, pressing into him, her hands circling his neck, bringing him closer. When she broke contact, she whispered against his lips. "I wish we could stay like this."

Maddox chuckled against her lips. "What, in an alley sitting on the cold hard ground?"

She sighed, nestling into his embrace. "In your arms. It is as close to heaven as I have ever imagined."

Maddox's hands closed on her shoulders and he pushed her far enough away to look down into her face. "Then stay with me. Don't go back to Trejikistan."

Her chin drooped and she pressed her forehead to his chest. "I cannot."

"Can't—or won't?" His tone hardened. When he'd

left her with Pierce, he'd known it was one of the biggest mistakes of his life. "Katya, in the short time I've known you, you've become such an amazing part of my life. You reminded me how good it feels to be alive." He tipped her chin up and gazed down into her eyes. "Stay," he said, his tone low, uncaring if the one word sounded like begging. He'd get down on his knees if he thought it would help.

A single tear rolled from the corner of her eye. "I have to go back. I have to do what has to be done."

Before he could question her further, an ambulance arrived, the sirens blaring and the lights flashing in their eyes.

Emergency medical personnel dropped down from the vehicle.

Pierce appeared before them. "I called the EMTs. Fulton needs attention, and I want them to have a look at you both."

Right behind the ambulance, a news van skidded to a stop, followed by another and another. Soon the alley looked like a celebrity mob scene.

The EMTs insisted on checking out Katya and Maddox. Between the reporters and the EMTs, Katya and Maddox were separated.

Maddox wanted to go to her, to protect her from the onslaught of the media.

A reporter stuck a microphone in Katya's face. "Is it true? You're not a terrorist? The weapons found in your apartment were planted by someone else?"

"Yes," Katya answered, standing on her toes, her gaze panning the crowd until she captured Maddox's.

Maddox mouthed the words, "Are you okay?"

She shrugged, a weak, unconvincing smile curling her lips.

People crowded around her, pressing so close, her eyes rounded, her hands coming up in a protective gesture.

Maddox shoved an EMT aside. "Thanks, but I'll live." He had to get to Katya.

As he pushed through the media, a reporter yelled out over the others, "Katya Ivanov, we have it from a good source that you are actually royalty from Trejikistan, Princess Alexi Katya Ivanov, next in line for the throne now that your father is dead and your brother is missing. Is that true?"

Katya gasped, tears welling in her eyes. She looked toward Maddox and back to the reporter. "No comment." She ducked her head, letting her hair fall over her face.

Maddox froze in place. Princess? Katya was a princess? How had he not known that? Surely the reporter had his facts wrong.

"Princess Alexi," another reporter pushed her way through the crowd gathering around Katya. "Are you seeking asylum in the United States since your government has been taken over in a military coup?"

Yet another reporter pressed in with his camera and microphone. "Princess, are you abandoning your country just when the people were on the verge of conducting their first democratic election?"

Maddox remained frozen in place, staring over the cameras and reporters to the woman trapped in the middle. Who was she? Did he even know?

Katya's head came up and she pushed her shoulders back. "I am not abandoning my country. As soon as I can get cleared to travel, I will return to Trejikistan and lead my people until the elections and the new democratic government is in place."

Pierce muscled his way beside Maddox. "We need to get her out of here."

When Maddox didn't move, Pierce frowned. "She didn't tell you, did she?"

All Maddox could do was shake his head. The woman he'd made love to, the woman he'd raced across the prairie with on the back of a snowmobile was a princess? "You knew?"

Pierce nodded. "She didn't want you to know. For what it's worth, she thought it would make you treat her differently. Does it change the way you feel about her?"

"Damn right."

"Take some time to digest it, brother. Don't do anything stupid." Pierce left his brother and pushed through the crowd. "Show's over. Leave the lady alone, she's been through enough."

Katya was loaded into an ambulance, Pierce climbing in beside her. Richard Fulton, under heavy FBI guard, left in another ambulance.

Maddox stayed where he was long after the ambulances and the press left the scene.

"Can I drop you off somewhere?" One of the remaining agents touched Maddox on the arm.

Until then, his mind had been somersaulting over everything that had happened in the past few days. When the agent brought him back to the present, his thoughts came together, one thing becoming crystal clear. He wanted to be with Katya. "Can you drop me off at the hospital?"

"Which one?"

"Whichever one they took the princess to." He ran toward the agent's vehicle and jumped in. When the agent didn't get right in, Maddox opened the door and called out. "Are you coming?"

The agent chuckled, sliding into the driver's seat. "Suddenly you're a man on a mission?"

"Damn right." A mission to find his princess.

Chapter Seventeen

"Thank God, you're alive!" Katya cried out in her native language. Propped against pillows in a sterile white hospital bed, she held Pierce's cell phone to her ear, tears of joy sliding down her cheeks.

"Yes, sister, I returned from Africa as soon as I could find transportation out," Dmitri said. "Vladimir had the armed forces mobilized to declare a military dictatorship, claiming the country would fall apart if he didn't take immediate action."

"Oh, Dmitri. What a horrible mess to come home to. I should have been there."

"Not to worry," he assured her. "I was able to avert disaster. As for the elections, everything is back on track."

"I am truly happy that you are alive and well." She dabbed at yet more tears. "Did you find out what really happened to Father?"

Dmitri paused. "Katya, Father was murdered. Cousin Vladimir is in prison. He confessed to hiring an assassin to murder our father."

"I know." Katya's fingers twisted her fingers around the pendant containing the tracking device that had almost gotten her killed. She had yet to give it up, and might never if she could find a way to destroy the device her father had implanted inside it to keep her safe. "They captured the assassin here."

"Excellent news."

"It's hard to believe Vladimir would kill his family for a throne," Katya said softly.

"I know." Her brother cleared his throat. "Speaking of news, word has come to us via the paparazzi that you have been busy yourself. What's this about your being a terrorist?"

Katya laughed. "It's a long story that I'll tell you all about when I arrive home. For now, I'm clear of all charges and free to leave whenever I get out of this hospital."

"Hospital? Are you well? Should I come to the United States to rescue you?"

"No, I am fine, just a few scratches and bruises, I promise I'll tell you all about it. If all goes well, I should be home in the next couple of days."

"Why?"

"Why? Don't you need me in Trejikistan?" She sat up, her brows furrowing.

"You are always wanted and needed, but everything is under control here. I do not know what you could add by returning. Father's funeral was today. The elections will take place soon and the monarchy will no longer be needed. If you want to stay in the United States, do so. I know it has always been your dream to lead a 'normal' life. Katya, this is your chance."

His words made her hands shake. "Are you sure?" Could it be that she would be free to lead her life just like anyone else? Free to choose where she could go?

Free of political functions and dull, formal meetings? Free to choose who she wanted to be with?

"Yes, Katya, my dear."

"What about you?" she asked. "What will you do?"

"I will be here until our people are comfortable with their new government. Then?" He laughed. "Perhaps I will join you."

Katya laughed, too, her heartbeat erratic, joy, elation and hope playing havoc with her ability to think. "I have to go."

"I love you, sister."

"And I love you." She pressed the End button and held the phone to her chest to keep her heart from jumping out.

Pierce Thunder Horse appeared in the doorway. "Good news?"

"The best!" When he reached for the phone, she couldn't help but hug him. "Thank you."

"For what? The use of my phone?"

"Yes!" She hugged herself and closed her eyes, afraid she was still dreaming and she'd wake up. She had to find Maddox. Katya opened her eyes and tossed the sheet off.

"Whoa, what's this?"

"I have to get out of here."

"You can't go anywhere."

"Am I still considered a terrorist suspect?"

"No, between the videos and Fulton's confession, you're off the hook."

She stood, holding the back of her hospital gown together. "Where are my clothes?"

"In the closet. But don't you think you should wait until the doctor releases you?"

"I can't wait." She ran for the closet, hauling her dirty clothes from the shelf.

Pierce captured her hands, clothes and all. "Could you wait at least until after one more visit?"

"I don't need another doctor to tell me what I already know. I'm fine. And I'll be even better when—"

"Not a doctor, a friend." Pierce turned her toward the door.

Maddox stood with a bouquet of deep red roses in his hand, a strangely shy expression on his face. "Katya." He stepped into the room, his gaze locked on hers.

"Maddox." Katya's breath lodged in her throat, her heart banging against her rib cage. She let Pierce take the clothes from her nerveless fingers and place them back on the shelf as she stood rooted to the floor.

"I see you two have a lot to talk about. I'll just leave you alone." Pierce pushed past Maddox and shut the door behind him.

When he didn't say anything, Katya cleared her throat and tried to tell herself not to get too excited. "What are you doing here? I thought you'd be on your way back to the ranch."

"No. I'm here to see you."

"The doctor did not find anything wrong. I can leave as soon as he signs my release papers."

Maddox took another step toward her, still holding the flowers. "That's what I wanted to talk to you about."

He was close enough for her to see the lines next to his eyes. Maddox looked tired and she wanted to reach out and stroke away the frown tugging his brows downward. "Did you want to talk about the doctor or my leaving?"

"Your leaving."

She swallowed, wondering how she could tell him she was not going back home without throwing herself in his arms and making a complete fool of herself. "About that…"

He closed the distance between them and pressed a finger to her lips. "No, let me have my say, then you can throw me out if you want."

"But I don't—"

He pressed his finger over her lips again. "Just listen."

She nodded and his hand dropped to his side. "I'm not sure how things work in your country. I don't speak the language and I'm not familiar with your protocol, but I'm willing to learn."

"Why are—"

"Shh, let me finish." He paced the floor, still carrying the bouquet in his hands. "What I'm trying to tell you…no, asking you…ah, hell." He stopped in front of her and held out the roses. "I want to be your bodyguard, or whatever it takes to be close to you. Don't you see? I want to get to know you. How you became a princess, your favorite color, when you lost your first tooth. Everything."

Tears welled up in Katya's eyes. Of all things he could have said, she'd never expected this, and she couldn't force words past the lump in her throat.

Maddox reached out to her, apparently realizing that he still held the roses. "These are for you."

She took the bouquet and held it up to sniff the fragrant petals.

His hands free, he wrapped them around her waist and pulled her close. "Don't you see? Crazy as it seems, I think I'm falling in love with you. Not the princess, not the political figure that could skate circles around my knowledge of protocol, but the passionate woman I first came to know in the cave. The warrior so much like my ancestors who's smart enough to know when to clobber a criminal with a two-by-four." He laughed. "So what do you think? Do you need another bodyguard? Think I could cut it in Trejikistan? I'm willing to go wherever you go."

Katya smiled and cupped his chin with her empty hand. "Maddox, look at me." When she had his attention, she told him her good news, "I'm not leaving."

His eyes widened. "You're not?"

"No. My brother is alive and well in Trejikistan. He'll take over all royal responsibilities. I'm not needed back home."

Maddox closed his eyes, sucked in a deep breath and let it out slowly. When he opened his eyes, a grin spread across his face. "Thank God. I really stink at foreign languages."

"Now that I'm not in line for the throne, I don't think I'll be needing a bodyguard, either."

His grin disappeared. "No?"

"No."

"Would you consider going on a real date with me?"

"To get to know you? Although we have been together pretty much nonstop for the past couple days, I do not know a lot about you." She smiled, her world a brighter place because of Maddox Thunder Horse. "I would be delighted to go on a date with you…on one condition."

His grin returned. "Name it."

"Don't call me Princess."

"Deal."

His dark eyes blazed, and he stood tall, his carriage that of a proud Lakota warrior. Then he bent to kiss her, his lips brushing gently against hers. "*Wankatanka yuha yuwakape miye.* The Great Spirit has blessed me."

* * * * *

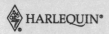 **HARLEQUIN®**

INTRIGUE

COMING NEXT MONTH

Available December 7, 2010

HICNM1110

REQUEST YOUR FREE BOOKS!

2 FREE NOVELS
PLUS 2
FREE GIFTS!

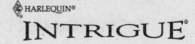

HARLEQUIN®
INTRIGUE®

Breathtaking Romantic Suspense

YES! Please send me 2 FREE Harlequin Intrigue® novels and my 2 FREE gifts (gifts are worth about $10). After receiving them, if I don't wish to receive any more books, I can return the shipping statement marked "cancel." If I don't cancel, I will receive 6 brand-new novels every month and be billed just $4.24 per book in the U.S. or $4.99 per book in Canada. That's a saving of at least 15% off the cover price! It's quite a bargain! Shipping and handling is just 50¢ per book.* I understand that accepting the 2 free books and gifts places me under no obligation to buy anything. I can always return a shipment and cancel at any time. Even if I never buy another book from Harlequin, the two free books and gifts are mine to keep forever.

182/382 HDN E5MG

Name	(PLEASE PRINT)	
Address		Apt. #
City	State/Prov.	Zip/Postal Code

Signature (if under 18, a parent or guardian must sign)

Mail to the **Harlequin Reader Service:**
IN U.S.A.: P.O. Box 1867, Buffalo, NY 14240-1867
IN CANADA: P.O. Box 609, Fort Erie, Ontario L2A 5X3
Not valid for current subscribers to Harlequin Intrigue books.

**Are you a subscriber to Harlequin Intrigue books and
want to receive the larger-print edition? Call 1-800-873-8635 today!**

* Terms and prices subject to change without notice. Prices do not include applicable taxes. N.Y. residents add applicable sales tax. Canadian residents will be charged applicable provincial taxes and GST. Offer not valid in Quebec. This offer is limited to one order per household. All orders subject to approval. Credit or debit balances in a customer's account(s) may be offset by any other outstanding balance owed by or to the customer. Please allow 4 to 6 weeks for delivery. Offer available while quantities last.

Your Privacy: Harlequin is committed to protecting your privacy. Our Privacy Policy is available online at www.eHarlequin.com or upon request from the Reader Service. From time to time we make our lists of customers available to reputable third parties who may have a product or service of interest to you. If you would prefer we not share your name and address, please check here. ☐

Help us get it right—We strive for accurate, respectful and relevant communications. To clarify or modify your communication preferences, visit us at www.ReaderService.com/consumerschoice.

HI10R

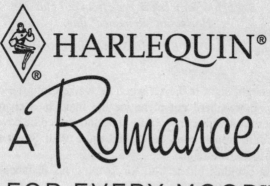

HARLEQUIN®

A Romance

FOR EVERY MOOD™

Spotlight on
Classic

Quintessential, modern love stories
that are romance at its finest.

See the next page
to enjoy a sneak peek from
the Harlequin® Romance series.

Introducing DADDY BY CHRISTMAS by Patricia Thayer.

MIA caught sight of Jarrett when he walked into the open lobby. It was hard not to notice the man. In a charcoal business suit with a crisp white shirt and striped tie covered by a dark trench coat, he looked more Wall Street than small-town Colorado.

Mia couldn't blame him for keeping his distance. He was probably tired of taking care of her.

Besides, why would a man like Jarrett McKane be interested in her? Why would he want to take on a woman expecting a baby? Yet he'd done so many things for her. He'd been there when she'd needed him most. How could she not care about a man like that?

Heart pounding in her ears, she walked up behind him. Jarrett turned to face her. "Did you get enough sleep last night?"

"Yes, thanks to you," she said, wondering if he'd thought about their kiss. Her gaze went to his mouth, then she quickly glanced away. "And thank you for not bringing up my meltdown."

Jarrett couldn't stop looking at Mia. Blue was definitely her color, bringing out the richness of her eyes.

"What meltdown?" he said, trying hard to focus on what she was saying. "You were just exhausted from lack of sleep and worried about your baby."

He couldn't help remembering how, during the night, he'd kept going in to watch her sleep. How strange was that? "I hope you got enough rest."

She nodded. "Plenty. And you're a good neighbor for

coming to my rescue."

He tensed. Neighbor? *What neighbor kisses you like I did?* "That's me, just the full-service landlord," he said, trying to keep the sarcasm out of his voice. He started to leave, but she put her hand on his arm.

"Jarrett, what I meant was you went beyond helping me." Her eyes searched his face. "I've asked far too much of you."

"Did you hear me complain?"

She shook her head. "You should. I feel like I've taken advantage."

"Like I said, I haven't minded."

"And I'm grateful for everything…"

Grasping her hand on his arm, Jarrett leaned forward. The memory of last night's kiss had him aching for another. "I didn't do it for your gratitude, Mia."

Gorgeous tycoon Jarrett McKane has never believed in Christmas—but he can't help being drawn to soon-to-be-mom Mia Saunders! Christmases past were spent alone…and now Jarrett may just have a fairy-tale ending for all his Christmases future!

Available December 2010,
only from Harlequin® Romance®.

HREXP1210